THE SEVEN SEALS

AND THE
SILVER LOCKET

A Star, A Shield and One Smooth Stone

CHARLOTTE TAYLOR

authorHOUSE®

AuthorHouse™
1663 Liberty Drive
Bloomington, IN 47403
www.authorhouse.com
Phone: 1 (800) 839-8640

Published by AuthorHouse 03/28/2018

ISBN: 978-1-5462-3568-2 (sc)
ISBN: 978-1-5462-3567-5 (hc)
ISBN: 978-1-5462-3566-8 (e)

Library of Congress Control Number: 2018903786

Print information available on the last page.

This book is printed on acid-free paper.

King James Version (KJV)
Scripture taken from The Holy Bible, King James Version. Public Domain

Acts 3:6
Silver and gold have I none, but, such as I have, give I thee

Acknowledgements

There are many people in my life that have inspired me in so many ways. To name them all would be impossible. To them I simple say thank you. My family has been very encouraging and forgiving of dinners not cooked. My sister Cindy has been my go to girl for information. Thanks for being so willing to share what you know. My work friends constantly ask how the book is going. Thanks to all of you. Dana, Timmy, Genessa, Danny, Kayla, Leigh, Dr. Turner, Alecia and Mattie. All of you have made the writing of this book more exciting to me. I think all of you can honestly say that this book is a living, breathing part of my life. Thank you all for not saying "shut up" every time I start talking about it.

Prologue

Old Mesilla, New Mexico. The shop didn't look like much on the outside but the silver jewelry on display in the window was enough to pull the customers in. Ande, short for Andrea, short for anyone at five feet, was not immune to such displays. Forever looking for 'the bargain', she pulled her reluctant husband Chase, who was forever trying to save money, into the shop.

"What could you possibly need now? I'll have to rent a U – haul just to get all the stuff you've already bought back home to Mississippi", the silver haired man looked down at his wife and with twinkling eyes began his old song and dance about the only way to save money is not to spend money. Ande, still pretty and petite at fifty - seven, with laugh lines around blue eyes and a mouth made for smiling, replied as usual.

"Yeah, yeah", as she looked from one jewel case to the other.

"I'm looking for Ashley's graduation present."

With a shake of his head Chase moved on to look around allowing his wife time to shop.

It takes a true shopper approximately five minutes to know whether a shop's contents are within her budget or not and this shop was a definite 'not'. Working her way around the counters toward the exit, Ande backed into a wall. Turning she found her wall to be a very large man with eyes as deep as the sea. She felt as if she were looking into the depths of heaven. The feeling was odd, not odd unpleasant but odd never the less.

"Oh, excuse me sir."

"May I show you something?" His voice reached in and touched her soul.

"No thank you, I'm just looking." Backing away, Ande began to look for Chase.

Smiling, the man held out his hand.

"This just came in today."

Wrapped in tissue paper was a beautiful silver locket necklace.

"The locket itself is silver but the charms inside are gold." He said.

As the thought 'Silver and gold have I none' filtered through her mind, Ande replied.

"It's beautiful, but I was just looking."

"It's a very old locket." Sea blue eyes twinkled.

"Let me be honest with you. It's worth more than I can afford. Thank you for showing it to me. It's beautiful." Looking around for Chase, Ande again began to back away.

"The previous owner is asking fifty dollars for the necklace."

"You're kidding!" And just that quick the shop Keeper connected to the 'bargain hunter' and sold a priceless locket for only fifty dollars. How very odd.

"It is said that the locket has a very interesting past. Would you care to hear about it?"

Hypnotic eyes looked deep into Ande's blue eyes.

Nodding her head Ande whispered.

"Yes please."

Chapter 1

"My name is Ashley and I have a story to tell."

The black cat's green eyes peered at the young girl in between licking her fur clean.

"My sister says I tell great stories so I feel very confident that you will find this story to be if not entertaining then at least educational. Feel free to laugh and cry with me as I remind you what it's like to be a teenager. What it's like to be different and why, to a teenager, that's not cool.

For a seventeen- year old I guess you could say my life is good. I have a nice home, clothes, plenty to eat, money to spend, popular at school and about to graduate. So, you're wondering how I'm different? I'm getting there. On a more personal level my life is a bust. How you ask? Well that's the problem. People are always looking at the package, the wrapping if you will. No one ever looks closer. No one ever looks past the wrapper. If they did they would see that I am just a mirage, a fake. I laugh and joke with my friends when actually I just want to sit and cry. I know there are many kids who feel as I do but seriously? I have my hands full just dealing with my crap. You know, like when you can't eat all your vegetables and your Mother says 'Eat! There are starving people in other Countries who would love to have what you have.' Don't you want to just say 'Well they can have it?' Yes, well, I can't deal with the starving people any more than I can deal with the many other kids who are going through what I am going through. My hands are full just getting through each day acting 'normal'. It's tiring, exhausting really. Let me give you an example.

My Parents are divorced. My two brothers and sister and I see our Dad frequently but it's not the same, you know? My Mother is a Nurse so her schedule is weird to say the least. In order to make sure we have what she thinks we need she works a lot. When she is not working she is running around with some of her Nurse buddies. My Dad really hurt her with his affair which is what tore our family apart so she has kinda gone off the deep end herself so to speak. We have our Grandparents, Nana and Papaw, and we are grateful but it's not the same, is it? Our Grandparents make sure we are taken care of and they take us to Church too. My sister and I are Believers and were baptized when we were younger. My youngest brother made a profession of faith and was baptized but acts as if he didn't. My other brother has not taken that step as yet. My Nana says that my Mom is a Believer. She chooses to ignore what's right, in order to live the life she wants right now. That doesn't make what my Mom is doing okay, so we pray for her every day that she will make better choices and that God will heal her hurts. Believing in God is one thing but I'm finding that living and reflecting that belief is another. Now that's my problem. Don't laugh, this is serious. I am in the twelfth grade, two months away from graduation. I have been reasonably popular as I have attended the same school all twelve years. I look alright. I mean I'm not beautiful but neither do I look like one of Cinderella's sisters either. You know, guys say I'm cute. My hair is chestnut brown, long, down to my bottom and thick and healthy looking. Your hair looks healthy too Kitty Kat. I have good skin, so my Nana has said. Yes, I know how lucky I am. I have a good friend who never wakes up without a new pimple on her face. She just hates her skin. My Mom says I have good genes. 'Say thank you she says'. Oh, to continue. I'm kind and I speak to everyone. I say 'yes ma'am and sir to adults and try to do right as much as I can. I am not perfect, for where is the fun in that, but I honestly do try to be good. Everyone looks at me as the nice Christian girl and treats me as such. They think I wrote the Bible and have all the answers. Ha! Ridiculous, right? Right. But it is what it is. Ok, so back to my being a fake. People think I have it all together, life I mean. They think I am the real deal. If truth be known, I thought so too. Here is what happened to show me and the world around me how so untogether I actually am.

This year we got a new History Teacher. It was very obvious his beliefs were different from my own and he made it his business to point out that his belief was superior to mine at every opportunity. He decided to have a debate on wars as our last project in History. We were to write about a war in History. It could be a past, present, or future war. We would then read our paper in class and then debate the whys and wherefores of the event with the presenter defending their paper as presented. In case things go south and the paper would be given two chances. Being the authority of the Bible as everyone thought, I chose to write about the Battle of Armageddon. I know, right? How utterly stupid and naïve can a person actually be and still be breathing. Well that's me. Even my Nana tried to talk me out of it. She kept saying my teacher was setting me up and that everyone could see me coming for half a mile away. She was right. My class did everything but sell tickets and what a show it was.

Well, just so you'll know, my paper was excellent. My Nana helped me and my facts and details were unequaled. My presentation was smooth. Where I got lost was my defense. With the encouragement of our Teacher, the class ripped me to shreds. It was a disaster. My hold on Biblical truth was wrenched from my cold lifeless fingers and sent swirling down the proverbial drain so to speak. I was a laughing stock. I could have had six monkeys doing a juggling act on my shoulders and would not have gotten more laughs. I was so mad I could have waged the battle of Armageddon right then and there in the class room with my Teacher taking the first direct hit. I walked out of that room thinking that all I knew about Christianity was zip, zero. One point for the pagans, zero points for the little Christian girl. All their thoughts hit me square in the back. 'You are a fake, a phony, not at all what we thought you were'. That's what brought me here to this point. Utter humiliation. That called for a talk with the Big Guy and for that I had to climb Mount Oak. That's what brought me here to this point Kitty Kat."

The sleek, black cat with the green eyes gave Ashley a look that said.

'Sorry… not interested', and she jumped from the tree into her back yard.

"Story of my life. I might as well be invisible."

Chapter 2

Ashley was out on a limb and she was as familiar with this position as she was with everything in her life. She ran her fingertips along the oak wood worn smooth by years of her sitting on this very branch.

Her Mother watched from the kitchen window and marveled at how easily she climbed the big old oak tree and laughed thinking about the poor trees on the college lawn that would be tested by her daughter in the coming fall.

"Mother, you should see Ashley sitting in her tree. It seems only yesterday she was six years old and climbing that big old tree for the first time. I was so scared she would fall out of the thing and break her neck that I begged her Dad to cut it down. Ashley threatened to run away from home if we cut her tree down. She says she talks to God from her limb. She says she feels she is in His face when she sits in her tree. Even then she knew how to get her way and still be so childish. She hasn't really changed. I'm not hurrying her or anything but she has to grow up some day. She's graduating in two months and then college. She seems so unsettled lately, more than usual, if you know what I mean, but she hasn't said anything. You know she doesn't talk to me. Has she said anything to you? I know she talks to you about everything."

Jana cradled the phone between her shoulder and ear to free her hands to peel potatoes, while she talked with her Mother.

"No, she hasn't said anything to me. Not lately anyway. You know they ripped her a new one in History class on her paper. That really bothered her."

"I told her not to write on Biblical stuff, people don't like that. She should have listened to me. You should have discouraged her."

4

"I tried to talk her out of it Jana but she is stubborn, just like you were at her age and now. She'll settle down. Graduation is a big event in her life. Oh, by the way, I got her graduation gift today. She's going to love it. I can't wait to tell you about it. It has the most amazing history and the man who sold it to me was amazing too."

Both women laughed because everyone knew Ande was crazy about her husband Chase. Ashley's Mother and Grandmother continued their conversation, comfortable with each other as mother and daughter should be.

Unaware of their conversation, Ashley was also thinking about graduation and college. She ran her fingers through her long brown ponytail, removing tree debris as she called it and allowed her thoughts to take an inward look.

"I'm scared Lord. I've lived at home surrounded by family and friends, gone to the same school and Church all my life. My whole existence has been right here. Once I start college all that will come to an end. How do I know that my beliefs are strong enough to carry me through college without my getting into trouble?"

Leaning her head back against the oak's trunk Ashley looked up unto the vast sky already growing dark with the coming storm. Her heart felt like a storm was growing there too.

"My Nana would say stand on the Bible and keep your eyes on Jesus."

Ashley rolled her eyes heavenward. Impatience guiding her movements she flung her left arm out.

"Easy to say but not always easy to do when keeping a low profile seems more prudent. Low profile you say?"

Ashley directs a laugh at herself.

"Yeah, right! After last week that no longer applies. Kinda like Leo from "Charmed" orbing himself out of a room full of people and hoping no one noticed."

Ashley frowned as she became serious.

"It seems part of me loves and believes in You and the other part questions so many things. Is that doubt? Is that being doubled minded? I hope not Lord. I need help. Will you help me Lord? You know what I'm talking about right? My grand about face in History class?

What happened last week in History class you ask? Well, let me tell you! I presented my paper on the Battle of Armageddon. I researched it, checked and double checked my time line, wrote it and studied it so that I knew all the facts. But something happened after I presented it. My brain went dead and Mr. Mercer and the class made mincemeat out of me. They trashed my paper and they trashed You. And the worst of it? I let them do it. I didn't defend my paper or You. Are You disappointed in me Lord? You should be. I'm disappointed in me. What does that mean? You said "If you deny Me before men, I will deny you before the Father". Please show me how to be strong. Please help me to know that I know that I am saved. I'm a little scared that if I can't stand up for you now for the little things, I won't stand a chance when the big things come along. What do You say Lord? Will you help me?"

Tired beyond belief Ashley closed her eyes and concentrated on the familiar sounds around her. The meows and growls of Kitty Kat and Bubba her next-door neighbor's cat and dog teasing each other. The comforting sounds of kids running and shouting at each other all around the neighborhood. The not so distant sounds of thunder in the night sky competing with Mr. Cole's TV program Fox News and her Mom's singing "Ain't No Mountain High Enough". Familiar and comforting sounds all of them but still the storm brewed in her heart. And then.

Several things happened at once.

Kitty Kat jumped into her lap.

"Kitty Kat!"

Her Mother called her from the kitchen door.

"Ashley, the storm is closer, you need to get out of the tree."

The lights went out all over the neighborhood.

There was a loud and close clap of thunder and the brightest light Ashley had ever seen all around her and then absolute and complete silence.

Chapter 3

It took one nanosecond to go from light to dark and I'm talking pitch black dark. Putting her hand in front of her face did not help her thundering heart one bit because she couldn't see her hand.

Several things occurred to Ashley all at once.

She was standing on her feet and not sitting on a branch in her oak tree or lying on the ground. The last thing she remembered was... was what? A bright light, yes, the light and she was alright, feeling for her arms and legs. Yes, she was definitely ok.

She also remembered the silence. Then....

Her breath hitched in her throat when she felt a whisper of movement close to her. She felt a chilling presence and... a voice.

"Hello, who's there?"

Ashley looked around but in absolute darkness she couldn't tell where the voice was coming from.

"Lord, where am I?" she whispered to herself as she replied in a slightly shaking voice.

"Who's there?"

"It must be an echo." The voice said sarcastically and close by.

"An echo?" Ashley looked everywhere with her arms outstretched.

"Now I know there's an echo." This time the whisper was louder and right in front of Ashley. Jumping back Ashley almost lost her balance.

"Are you a friend or an enemy?" She whispered between chattering teeth as she balanced herself.

"It depends." Came the amused reply.

"On what?" Ashley asked in astonishment.

"On whether or not you are friend or enemy, and why are you whispering?" This was said with laughter ringing around what sounded like an empty room.

"I am definitely a friend and I have no clue where I am or how I got here, and I don't know why I'm whispering. I was sitting in my oak tree one minute and the next I'm standing in the dark. Where are we and are we alone? I thought I felt another presence here before you spoke."

Ashley still couldn't see and believe me she was trying to see the girl she was talking to. At least she thought it was a girl, in the pitch dark even sounds were distorted.

"I don't know the answer to either of your questions. My memory is a little vague on details right now for some reason."

"Ohhhh" a whisper of movement and then.

Ashley screamed as someone touched her arm.

"Let me go!"

"Hey! Cool it Goldilocks. You made the hair stand up and salute on my arms with that scream. I didn't know you were so close or I would have warned you."

Suddenly Ashley felt another chill wash over her and she began to shake. Moving forward she bumped into the girl.

"Geeze Louise, are you a vampire, like from 'Twilight'? Your arm is cold as ice."

"A vampire? Hardly, I'm a senior at Patrick Valley High School. I'm scared to death. Aren't you scared? Hey! Did you feel that?"

Ashley felt as if someone or something walked close to her. Just a whisper of movement with a touch of evil.

"What?"

"That….." Somehow knowing this girl would never understand, Ashley whispered "Never mind."

"A senior huh. What do ya know? Me too. That is, I'm a senior and I'm scared too."

"Really? Where?"

"Where? Oh, you mean school. I don't know. Like I said, I'm a little short of details right now. I'm not sure about anything. I guess finding myself here from where ever I was, has short circuited my brain."

"Well, there was an electrical storm. Do you know who you are? I'm Ashley."

"Ashley, that's pretty. I'm Paige. It's funny that I remember my name but nothing else huh?"

"Well Paige, your name sounds familiar. I'd shake your hand except I can't see your hand or mine for that matter; which brings me back to our problem. Where are we and how did we get here? I think the lights went out in my neighborhood. I don't remember you living there but there are new folks coming and going all the time. Neighborhoods are like that. This doesn't feel like my neighborhood, so where are we and how do we get back? That is if we are somewhere that is not home. Could this, be a dream? If it is, whose dream is it, yours or mine?"

"Ashley, would you be offended if I asked you if I could hold your hand? Just so we don't lose each other. I'm standing close to you but I can't see any part of you."

"Good idea. No offense taken. What is that?" Ashley's breath hitched up a notch as somewhere in the distance she could see a light.

"Is that a light?" Asked Ashley.

"Yep. That's a light alright."

"Should we go to it? It's a little frightening considering we don't know where we are and all."

"Maybe we're dead and just need Melinda."

"Melinda?"

"Girl don't you watch TV? Melinda Gordan??? 'The Ghost Whisperer'? Gee girl you need to loosen up a little." A laugh built into Paige's voice and it tumbled out loud and clear.

"The best I can do is…. 'Don't go into the light'. Ha ha. But still, Paige, where are we and what is that light?" Tears began to gather in Ashley's eyes and as the tears fell the light began to come closer.

"Uh oh. I don't think we have a choice about going into the light. It's going into us. Maybe we are dead." Paige's voice was a little wobbly which was comforting. It made Ashley feel better to know she was not the only one afraid here.

"It's not supposed to happen this way you know, death I mean."

"How do you know? Have you died and experienced death then lived to tell about it?" This was said with a smirk.

"No but I do know what the Bible says about it. And this isn't it."

"The Bible! You aren't one of those are you? You definitely need to get a life." There was definitely a smirk in that question.

"A Christian you mean? Yep and I have a life thank you very much!"

"Ashley! The light!" With a scream, the two girls hug each other as they find themselves bathed in the brightest light either had ever seen. The light was so bright it blinded both girls so that they each had to close their eyes to block the pain of going from pitch black to total light. Frightened out of their minds the girls hung on to each other afraid to let go for fear of the unknown. Neither girl questioned the fact that they had just met under very weird circumstances and yet, they were acting as if they had known each other all their lives. Their eyes stayed shut, afraid of what they would see if they opened them. They also stayed quiet not making a sound in case someone else was there that might hurt them. One praying for strength to face the unknown, the other just trying to muster the courage to open her eyes. Both of them admitting that their goose was probably cooked.

Chapter 4

"Ashley, Paige, you can open your eyes now." The voice was like music. It filled the soul with hope, confidence, and security.

Ashley opened her eyes and looked into the bluest eyes she had ever seen, eyes that had seen everything but were still filled with hope. Eyes that were deep as the soul and just as fathomless as the ocean. Eyes that filled her with quiet joy and great fear at the same time.

"Are we in Heaven?" she asked softly.

"Yes." One word but that was all it took for Paige.

"We're dead? We can't be. I'm not a Believer. I don't believe in GOD or Heaven. And I don't believe in you either, whoever you are." Anger filled her and she all but stamped her foot.

"Hold on, you're not dead but you are in Heaven." Then he smiled.

Paige started to speak but Ashley interrupted her.

"If we're not dead, what are we doing in Heaven?"

"Ashley, you do need to get a life! You can't seriously be serious. THERE IS NO SUCH THING AS HEAVEN! Grow up and smell the... is that food?" Paige's attention was diverted by a woman dressed like an amazon in a white tunic trimmed in gold with a plate of something that smelled heavenly. She offered the plate to Paige who shamelessly helped herself. Ashley's eyebrows raised a little as she looked at Paige taking food from the tray.

"A girl's gotta eat." She reminded Ashley of the little beast in the movie 'Spiderwick' who was so often diverted by the birds flying about. She couldn't help herself as she whispered to Paige.

"Pretty Birds."

Ashley looked up into the man's blue eyes again and thought how deep is the sea? Sea? What is the matter with her?

"If we are not dead, what are we doing in Heaven?" she asked again. Ashley did not register the fact that she was accepting this man's explanation of Heaven.

"Answering your request." Glancing at Paige he laughed. The sound was like tinkling glass wind chimes.

"Answering my request or Paige's request?" She too looked over at Paige who was eating fluffy white things and groaning as if they were the answer to a food lover's prayer.

"Both." He motioned for her to try the white fluffy food as well. It was good, it was like eating all her favorite foods.

"Yummm, manna." She breathed.

"Yes." The man turned and started walking away.

"Wait!" Ashley called. The man stopped and motioned for Ashley and Paige to follow. Paige grabbed more of the fluffy white stuff, handed some to Ashley and said.

"Let's go."

"If we're going to be following you around shouldn't we at least know your name?"

"Michael."

"Right," grunted Paige. "Listen Ashley, you're not really falling for this song and dance, are you? She turns to Michael.

"Listen dude," grabbing his sleeve Paige looks him in the eye.

"My friend here doesn't get out often so go easy on her she doesn't recognize a phony when she sees one."

"And you do? What's that you're eating?" Paige pulls a morsel out of her mouth.

"Ahhh I get it. You've doctored the food and we're taking a ride in fairy land, is that it?" About to throw the food down Michael stops her with his words.

"And your ride started with the dark, am I right? I think that was before you ate the fairy food."

Paige had the grace to look ashamed.

"Oh yeah, my Mom always said I had more imagination than anyone needed."

"You remembered something Paige. My Mom says the same thing about me. Michael, really, where are we, what are we doing here and how do we get home and why do I want to trust all that you've said?" Ashley touched his tunic sleeve as she waved her other arm to encompass the here and now.

"Ashley, Paige, you are in Heaven and you're here because GOD wills it and as for getting home..." Michael turns toward Paige as she interrupts.

"Here it comes Ashley, the rest of the bull but he's walking in tail first."

"You know, I thought I knew all there was to know about patience, being an archangel and all but that was before I met you Paige." Suddenly there was thunder everywhere.

"Sorry Father."

Ashley laughs. "Just like in the movies."

"Not quiet. Let me show you something." Michael turns to a pedestal with a solid gold treasure chest sitting on top. The lid was on the marble floor. Both girls look inside at the same time and bump heads. With an exclamation and head rubbing both girls say "there's a book in there!" at the same time.

"what else was in it?" asked Paige.

"Jewels?" asked Ashley.

"Look closer. This is the book with the Seven Seals. The Seven Seals are gone." Michael calmly looks from one girl to the other.

"As in the flippered wet kind?" said Paige, smirking again.

"As in the who is worthy to open kind?" asked Ashley timidly.

"The very ones, someone stole them."

"Ok now I know we aren't in Heaven as if I ever believed it was possible in the first place. No one but no one steals from GOD, if I believed there was a GOD which I don't." Taking a deep breath Paige's look definitely says I told you so.

"She's right, no one steals from GOD." Ashley looks at Michael with an explain yourself look.

"People steal from GOD all the time. Ask the Treasurer of your Church if you don't believe me."

"Well yeah, but here in Heaven?"

"Ashley!"

"Give it a rest Paige. We're certainly not in Kansas anymore."

"I'm from Mississippi, thank you very much."

"Me too, but we're not there either. Ok Michael, I don't know how anyone could steal something from right here in Heaven, under GOD's nose if you will, but I'll bite. What has that got to do with Paige and myself?"

"GOD says you two are the only ones who can find the Seven Seals."

"Paige and me? I don't know about her but I can't even find clothes to wear to school."

"And I still get lost going to the bathroom." Paige frowned at me.

"Hey, me too."

"Never the less it's you two."

"But wait a minute." Ashley looks at Michael questioningly. "The Bible says Jesus is the only one worthy to open the Seven Seals so what good was it for someone to steal them and how did they get them from the Book without the Book opening?"

"That's very true. Only Jesus can open the Seals. The Seven, silver Seals resting on top of the Book were taken, the Seals were not broken. But stolen, Jesus can't open them and the seven years of tribulation will be delayed, the last battle won't be fought and satan..."

"He can't win, can he?" Tears gathered in Ashley's eyes. Michael gives Ashley a hug.

"No, he can't win. All will be well little one. You and Paige will find the Seals and return them to their rightful place. GOD has confidence in you and much to my surprise, so do I."

"Ashley tell me you're not buying into this ridiculous story." Paige pulls Ashley to stand in front of her. "Well?"

Ashley looks at Michael and then at Paige. Then Ashley looks at the gold box.

"Paige?" Ashley begs Paige with her look.

"No Ashley, this is just a dream. A nightmare actually. We're both just having a dream. I'm having a humdinger of a bad dream. But why dream of Heaven? It's not real, it's not real. I'll just click my heels together three times and say….'there's no place like home, there's no place like home."

"Settle down Dorothy." Ashley begins.

"Paige…" Michael begins.

"Pay no attention to that man behind the curtain." Paige begins. Michael laughs long and heartily.

"Your Mother was right. You do have more imagination than you need."

"The TV was my babysitter."

"Paige, we would have been good friends back home if we had known each other. Do we know each other?" Looking at Michael Ashley then says.

"So, what do we do now Michael? Where do we start? And before you say it Paige, not at the yellow brick road. What exactly are we looking for, can you get us started because I haven't got a clue what to do. We need to get this done because my Mother will be looking for me soon. There's a storm coming and my Mother will be worried."

"Ashley, the storm has just started so listen carefully."

"Yes, I'm all ears too Auntie Em." Paige was all sarcasm.

With a chuckle Michael turns to another amazon type woman in a white tunic trimmed in emerald green. Laughing out right at the irony of the green trim and oz.

"You'll need these clothes. Keep your hair covered at all times with this head covering. In this bag is manna, there is enough food to last. The bag never gets empty. Sandals for your feet, oh and watch where you step. Be careful what you say, you don't want to change history. Don't worry about the difference in the language, you'll understand them and they'll understand you. You are looking for a round silver Seal. You'll know it when you see it. If you get into trouble just call my name and I will be there. Keep your heads and wits about you at all times. I must warn you that someone else wants the Seals as bad as you do and he'll do anything to get them. Remember GOD would not give you this task if HE for one minute, thought you couldn't accomplish it. Call me if you need me."

"Call you? But you didn't give us a phone." Paige looked puzzled.

With those words and one last look Michael was gone.

"Where did he go? Oh Paige, you look so funny." Ashley laughs at the picture Paige makes in her outfit.

"Honey have you looked in the mirror lately? I don't remember putting this on. Course I don't remember a lot of things lately. So, what's next? Where do we go from here? I can't believe I'm doing this. Where did he say for us to look for the Seal things?" Paige turns to Ashley as she hears her clear her throat.

"Where did this door come from? I don't remember. Oh what the heck. After you."

Ashley looks at Paige and with a sigh she says.

"Paige, my Mother is going to be so upset with me. Do you think she'll be worried?" Tears ran down her cheeks.

"It'll be alright Ashley. I can't remember much about my home but we're just dreaming anyway. We'll wake up any minute, you'll see."

Ashley opens the door. She and Paige step through into darkness.

"Ohhh!" they both say in unison.

Chapter 5

As two sets of small feet hit the ground, the dark surrounded them like a blanket. The cold night air tried to seep through their clothes to chill their skin. Fog was settling in patches low to the ground. Ashley shivered violently.

Paige looks around seeing dark shadows and the light from the huge moon hitting the fog in places making the shadows look threatening and then feeling a cold breeze on her face making her shiver with fear.

"This definitely looks like vampire country." Paige said between her own chattering teeth.

"Do you even have one serious bone in your body? Must you always crack jokes about everything? Paige, we are in serious trouble here. Aren't you scared? It's dark, it's cold, it's foggy, we're lost, I'm sleepy and I want to go home. I don't know how to be a detective, I don't know how to find things, I'm scared out of my mind and just the thought of this being vampire country makes me grind my teeth!" Ashley started to cry.

"Don't cry Ashley. I'm sorry. I always make jokes when I don't know what to say or when I'm nervous. I'm scared too. All this is so unbelievable. Look at the moon. Isn't it beautiful? If you close your mind to all that has happened you can almost imagine that we are home, wherever that is. Here the moon looks mystical, magical, beautiful and just down right perfect. Where are we now do you suppose?" Paige looked around as wet fog drifted across her face.

Lifting her small face up to the sky, Ashley feels the cold air dry the tears on her cheeks. Her mother always said she had an expressive face and could never hide her emotions. Regret was plainly written across her beautiful features as she said...

"I don't know. I feel so far from my mother. We haven't always gotten along. My mother's lifestyle isn't exactly what the Lord had in mind when he established the family. You know, mom and dad at home with the kids. She is never at home, her friends at work seem more important. Of course, dad's not there because they are divorced but he wasn't there even when they were married. I guess I've been pretty vocal about it and that creates arguments between my mom and me. My grandparents raised my mom. It's not right for them to have to raise their grandkids too. It's pretty hard on my brothers and sister too. I guess I haven't been the example the Lord intended me to be and now I might not have another chance to show my mother how much God loves her. My cousin just got married and his new wife, Melissa and daughter Melanie, are so sweet. I wanted to get to know them better and thinking I may not get that chance makes me so sad."

"What about your dad? Where is he?"

"My dad. Now there is a question. He left. He had other priorities that didn't include his family. It's okay though. I don't leave him out of my prayers. I see him now and again but, I don't need him. I feel as if he abandoned us. Like, we weren't enough for him, not important enough. For a long time, I blamed myself for dad leaving us, but not anymore. That's his sin, not mine. Divorce is not the unpardonable sin, but I wonder how many prayers from how many kids has the Lord had to listen too. I wonder how he has dealt with all the heartbreak, the sadness, the tears, and the utter feeling of lostness. I feel sorry for my dad because he has some great kids. He has missed so much and is not even aware of it. My feet are so cold in these wet sandals."

Bending down and touching the ground Ashley whispers.

"Grass! We're standing on grass. It's wet. Wonder what time it is here. What is that just ahead there? Come on Paige, let's look." Ashley starts walking.

"Wait Ashley." Paige tries to grab Ashley's arm but Ashley was already out of reach.

"It's a bush." Ashley does a slow complete turn, looking everywhere. Bushes dotted what looked like a large hill. Looking at the sky and again at her surroundings, Ashley grabs Paige's hand and shouts, it's a mountain Paige! We're on a mountain! Come on, let's go up this hill and look around.

Did you hear something?" Ashley looks around trying to see through the fog and night air.

"No but what is that smell?" Paige scrunches her nose and shakes her head.

"Bells! I hear bells. Come on Paige I think I hear music. It sounds strangely familiar."

Pulling Paige by the arm Ashley begins walking up the hill toward the sounds of music and tinkling bells. Then another sound stops them both dead in their tracks.

"Baaaaa"

"What in the world….."

"Baaaa, baaaa, baaaa"

Following the sound around the hill both girls nearly fainted at the sight before them.

Hiding behind a large bush both girls stare in absolute amazement.

A teenage boy was sitting beside a large fire surrounded by sheep. He was running his hand along strings on a bent bow that resembled a crude musical instrument. The sound he was making was pleasant to the ears and better than some instruments the girls had heard at home. His voice was soothing as he crooned a rather odd but familiar song to his flock of sheep.

"Calm little lambs, don't be afraid

Your shepherd is here

Don't be afraid

Rest for awhile

Tomorrow is near

I'm keeping watch

No need to fear…."

Paige grabs Ashley's arm and points toward the teenager.

"Ashley, do you see what I see?"

"Yes, you don't think we are in Australia, do you?"

"Paige, believe it or not, I think I've seen this boy before. The déjà vu thing."

"I know. He looks like he is wearing a short dress or something. Scotland? Uh oh!"

The teenager laid his instrument down and quick as a flash he picked up a sword and a shield and stood before the fire like an avenging angel.

The shadow of the boy was reflected by the fire onto a huge boulder behind him giving his image a larger than life, Indiana Jones quality that sent shivers down both girls' spines.

"Come out into the open where I can see you, man or beast. These are my sheep, in my protection and I will fight for their safety. Come out now or I will come for you."

"Please, hold your fire, your sword, whatever. We mean your sheep no harm. We are lost and can't find our way…."

"Ashley did you just quote from…."

"Paige!"

Turning toward the teen Ashley tries to be brave.

Who are you and where are we?"

Ignoring Ashley's question the boy motions toward the girls.

"Come into the light so that I might see you clearly. If you have weapons I warn you not to try anything. The Lord is on my side and I will protect myself and my sheep at all costs." The young man swung his sword aggressively at the girls.

Stumbling over large rocks the girls tumble to a heap at the guy's feet. He jumped back as if the girls were snakes and pointing his sword at them. The young man demanded in a firm, confident tone.

"Who are you and what do you seek?"

"We are lost. We do not mean you or your sheep any harm. Would you tell us please where we are?"

"You did not tell me who you are."

"I'm Ashley and this is Paige. Please, where are we?"

"Bethlehem"

Ashley looked shocked as she said…

"Bethlehem!" from her seat on the ground.

Paige held center stage as she jumped gracefully to her feet growling.

"Bethlehem! Somebody please, just give me a break. I have about had it. This is not Bethlehem, there is no God, Michael or lost seals. I am not standing in the middle of a mountain pasture full of sheep defending myself from a guy in a dress wielding a sword. Smelling. What is that smell anyway? I am asleep and please, somebody pinch me and wake me up when this nightmare is over!" Paige's body was trembling from the effort to keep herself from screaming. She flung herself down onto the wet grass and with her head on her knees she moans…

"And for crying out loud, did it really have to be smelly sheep?"

Ashley and the strange young man looked down at Paige in astonishment.

"Is she alright?" asked the guy in a quiet voice.

"She will be." Ashley bent down and gently pinched her.

"Ouch!"

"We have had an extraordinary day, all in all." Ashley's hand was patting Paige's shoulder.

"She wasn't truthful about God." Said the quiet voice.

"I know, but it is what she believes. Is this really Bethlehem?" Ashley sweeps her hand around the surrounding area.

"Bethlehem? Yes, I love it here, so quiet, err… it was quiet before you two came. And why did you come here? My sheep sense no danger in your presence so I will remove my sword but beware, I will watch you closely." The young man placed his sword and wooden shield beside a rock close to the fire.

Trying to decide what to say to the young man about why they were here at this place, Ashley helped Paige to stand and quietly asked her.

"Are you okay?"

Paige hiccoughed and nodded.

Ashley walked closer to the fire as the cold seeped right down to her bones. Looking around at the sheep Ashley looked at the teenager and said.

"If this is really Bethlehem, and this is really sheep, then who are you?"

The young man stood straight and with a regal look said.

"I am David, son of Jesse, the Bethlehemite."

Both girls stood as if turned to stone. They looked once at each other and then, as in one voice exclaimed.

"King David!"

Chapter 6

David stood straight and tall, looking for all intents and purposes the King the Bible proclaimed him to be. Ruddy complexion, beautiful eyes, handsome appearance, pure of heart, obedient and strong of faith. David was wearing a smock type outfit tied at the waist with a large piece of string, sandals on his dirty feet and dirt on his handsome face. The shock of seeing David and hearing him identify himself and knowing him to be one of the most talked about Bible characters caused both girls to stand with their mouths opening and closing like fish out of water. Their obvious shock and silence cleared the air for David. He bent and picked up his sword and shield and took on an exaggerated stance with his sword crossed in front of his wooden shield, chin in the air he bowed deeply and proclaimed in a loud voice.

"Welcome strangers to my kingdom. My loyal subjects." He waved his sword in the direction of the sheep. "Have all gathered near to welcome you as well. My land extends as far as the eye can see, at least you could see if it wasn't so foggy and you both may consider my home to be your home. We are atop a mountain so please don't go wandering off on your own, you might find yourself with a broken leg or worse at the bottom of a drop off. There are also wild and dangerous animals who pounce and devour."

Both girls looked around at the grassy mountain plateau with terrified faces as David continued.

"Please don't address me as King David, you both must call me David, my subjects the sheep would not know to whom you are talking to, you see, they might get confused. Please forgive my lack of formal dress and the lack of a banquet to welcome you as I was not expecting guests. The sheep and I have grown slack in the weeks since we arrived to this area of our kingdom. We don't have many guests you see."

The stunned look on both girls' faces along with the smell of him and his sheep reaching their noses was the straw that broke the camel's back for David. He dropped his sword and shield to the ground laughing loud and heartily.

"You should see your faces! They are as funny as your thinking I am a King. You haven't seen many Kings I take it or you would not have voiced such a statement. Me a King? I, am only seventeen."

David was interrupted by a tiny lamb butting his leg with her head. The lamb was small and white with a black face and black feet. She stood with her head up, tail wagging and looking at David as if he were the king of her world.

"Joy, you think I'm a king, don't you?" David bent to rub her head much to her obvious pleasure.

The lamb captured both girls' attention.

"Joy! What a perfect name for her. How cute she is. She is trying to get your attention. Look at her Paige. She knows we are watching her. Look at her prance."

Ashley clapped her hands together in her excitement. The abrupt noise startled the flock of sheep and they began to move in closer to David, butting and bumping into the girls and would have trampled the little lamb, had David not scooped her up into his arms. Most of the sheep were large, wooly and smelled dirty. As the girls jumped from one encounter to the other, the sheep began to get pushy. Ashley and Paige didn't know which direction to go in. They were getting hit from every side by angry sheep.

"David!" both girls shouted at once.

"Don't move!"

In an instant David had his crudely made musical instrument in his arms and was playing the loveliest tune the girls had ever heard, as he sat on a large rock. His quiet voice instructed the sheep to settle down. In a flash, the sheep stopped moving and began to lie down, closing their eyes for sleep. Both girls took a deep breath and looked at David for direction.

"The sheep trust me, I'm their shepherd. They rely on me and enjoy hearing my voice and my music. To my sheep, I represent peace and plenty. When they hear my voice, they are reassured of my care and affection.

They feel safe and are able to settle down." David was not bragging but simply stating fact.

"Now." David looked at the girls inquiringly.

"Who are you and what are you doing on my mountain. I know neither of you are from Bethlehem."

Chapter 7

Paige looked to Ashley to answer David's questions. Ashley took a deep breath and began.

"We are from far, far away. We were sent to Bethlehem on a mission. We were sent by God to find one of the Seven Seals taken from Heaven. We don't know who took them or why. There are seven altogether and who knows where they are or how we are supposed to find them but God thinks we can. I believe in God but Paige doesn't. Neither one of us knows how to find things but we can't go home until we find those Seven Seals of Revelation, and they may be here in Bethlehem somewhere. Paige and I want to go home you see and we were hoping you would be able to help us. Since you are here I think God is letting us know you are somehow involved."

David looked outraged and exclaimed as he jumped to his feet.

"I would never... never steal from God. The Lord is my Shepherd and I have never wanted for anything. Why, He is my rod and my staff. Why would I steal from Him? You must be mistaken!"

David looked every inch the King.

"No David, you have misunderstood what Ashley is trying to say." Paige said quietly, mindful of the sheep beginning to get restless again.

"Ashley meant that God, at least who she thinks is God, wants you to help us find the Seals, at least one of them. She did not mean to imply that you had anything to do with or was involved in the taking of the Seals from Heaven or where ever they were to start with. Oh snap! You can help us find them, can't you?"

"I find lost sheep. Maybe I can find lost seals."

Both girls burst into laughter. It was plain that David had no idea what he said or why the girls were laughing so hard.

"You are laughing at me."

David's chin went up and a glint came into his eyes.

Ashley stopped laughing with some difficulty.

"Well you see David, in our country there are animals called seals. They live in the water and have flippers. We also have sheep. So, when you said you find lost sheep and maybe could find lost seals, we connected the two and found it very funny. We were laughing at what you said not at you."

Ashley began to laugh again.

"So, we need to find water to find your seal?" David sounded eager.

"No, our lost Seal isn't an animal. It's an object. Paige and I have never seen one but Michael said we would know it when we saw it."

"Who is Michael?"

"God's Arch Angel."

"You've seen God?" this was said with reverence.

"No but we have seen Heaven and the Arch Angel Michael."

Paige jumped up.

"I've had about as much of this as I can take. For the last time! There is no God, Heaven or Angels. We are dreaming and right now I'd say it is turning into a nightmare. I am so tired I could fall asleep standing up. Can't we talk about this in the morning?"

Paige began to run her hands through her short brown hair.

David looked at Paige with concern.

"She's jesting about not believing in God, surely. God is our rock, our salvation, the God of Abraham, Jacob and Isaac. His lovingkindness is everlasting. Blessed be the Lord, the God of Israel."

"Wow! It's one thing to read it but quite another to actually hear it."

David looked puzzled.

"I'm thinking I am the one dreaming and not able to wake up. You girls are strange. Your names, Ashley, Paige, they are strange names. Not ones we use here. But as you say, you are not from here."

Paige stopped running her hands through her hair and looked first at Ashley and then at David.

"I'm so tired Ashley, aren't you?" Tears were bright in her eyes but unshed.

David began to clean around a large boulder close to the fire. He pulled blankets out of a knapsack and spread them on the ground. He turned to the girls and said.

"Lay here close to the fire. We need to settle for the night."

Paige looked at David in shock once again.

"Settle for the night? Here? What do you mean?"

"I mean we have to sleep close to the fire because it gets cold up in the mountains at night."

David's tone of voice was soft and gentle so as not to startle the sheep.

Paige, however, did not feel the need to keep her voice low.

"You surely don't mean we are going to sleep outside in the cold. Ashley, we can't sleep outside. I don't do the camping thing. It smells, and the sheep are pushy and probably infested with, I don't know, creepy, crawly, itchy things. There is dirt on the ground and wet grass and I have to go to the bathroom and I don't know where it is. I really need to go home but I can't remember where that is either but I know I came from somewhere. Didn't I? Yes, of course I did. We need to just go. Now! Ashley?"

Paige began to turn in circles not knowing which direction to go in. Suddenly she was on the ground looking up at the little lamb in shocked silence. The lamb had butted Paige's legs knocking her flat on the seat of her pants. Joy's long wet tongue came out and all at once was on Paige's face. Paige began to cry.

"Finally. I was beginning to think you were a robot with one switch. The wisecracker switch. It's great to know you don't have all the answers. Now, stop crying and let's take care of first things first. David, we need to go to the little girl's room, can you direct us?"

Ashley looked back at David as she pulled Paige to her feet.

It was David's turn for his mouth to fall open.

"The little girl's room? Look around you, there's room for all God's little girls here."

David laughed and punched a large wooly sheep as if he were sharing a joke.

"No, I mean the bathroom. Where is your bathroom?"

Ashley put her hands on her hips in agitation.

"Bathroom? What is that?"

David mocked her actions, hands on his hips.

Paige cut in.

"For a future King, you sure are short on smarts."

David laughed again.

"Smarts? King? Bathroom? I don't understand. Where do you two come from? Not Bethlehem you say. Egypt? I hear people there are strange. Explain yourself."

David folded his arms across his chest and waited like an impatient parent except his foot did not tap.

"Bathroom is where we go to relieve ourselves. I guess you go in the bushes."

Ashley looked uncomfortable.

"Yes, bushes."

David also looked uncomfortable.

"Don't wonder too far. There are wild animals on this mountain."

"Are you coming Paige?"

Ashley looked at the fog closing in.

"Forget it I'll wait."

Frustrated, Paige flopped down to the ground, pushing away a sheep who wanted to sit in her lap.

"Not me." Ashley looked down at Paige and then gave David a don't start with me look, then...

Ashley marched off into the fog.

"I'll be back." And she was gone. Swallowed up by the thick, gray fog.

Chapter 8

Ashley looked around, careful not to get too far from David's camp. The fog made it difficult to see much but she found a large stone and hoping there were no snakes she sat down. Elbows on her knees, chin in her hands, Ashley let her tears fall. She cried for herself, for Paige and for their families who she knew must be worried sick wondering where they were. Her eyes were closed and she knew she had to look a mess. Wishing for a damp wash cloth, Ashley felt a moist puff of air hit her face and then before she could scream a wet sloppy tongue went across her eyes, licking the last of her tears away. Surprise and fear had her eyes popping open, looking into soft brown eyes set into a black face.

"Joy!"

The lamb recognized her name because she pranced around playfully. Coming close to Ashley the little lamb looked up into her eyes. A question was clearly hanging in the air.

"Oh Joy, you must be a wonderful delight to David. Does he know you have wandered off, away from the fire? He'll come searching for you soon I think."

Joy pressed her face into Ashley's hands, pushing close to her.

"Oh, you little dear!" Ashley placed a kiss on her nose.

"Okay, get up here. You and I can have a nice long chat. I'll talk and you can listen. Deal? Deal."

Placing her back against the tree that Ashley discovered was next to the rock, she made herself and Joy comfortable.

"Where do I start baby Joy? I'm seventeen. Hoping to live to be eighteen. I'll be graduating from High School in two months, did you know that? Yep. I've attended the same school since the first grade."

Joy yawned.

"Boring, I know this to be true, but that's me."

Joy grunted.

"Popular you ask? I guess so. That is everyone likes me. What's not to like? I'm not the leader of the pack or anything like that, just well liked. At least the girls like me. The boys are a different story. I go to church and everyone knows I'm a Christian, so I get asked out by the guys I go to church with. But I usually don't go because I'm not comfortable dating just yet. But you don't care about that, do you Joy baby?"

Joy licked her hand and Ashley laughed and began to softly rub her head.

"My home life has been difficult. My Dad decided his home, his wife and kids weren't enough for him and he started looking somewhere else. My Mother was devastated. As a result, she doesn't have anything to do with men now. I think she is guarding her heart from further hurt and pain. But in the process, she has made terrible decisions that have affected all of us. I have made her life worse by being a pain at every opportunity and now I fear that I might never get another chance to tell her how much God and I love her. Mostly, I want to tell her that I'm sorry."

A sob caught in Ashley's throat.

Joy rubbed her head back and forth across Ashley's hands.

"You're well loved, aren't you Joy girl? I bet David tells you all the time how much he loves you. I know I would if I had you at home. Home. Do you think I'll ever see my home again Joy? Is Paige right? Are we dreaming? Paige. Where did she come from? She's familiar, yet she's a stranger. I feel like I've known her forever, but I never met her until I bumped into her in the dark. We're becoming close friends, but I think part of that has to be the circumstances we've found ourselves in. And, what about her memory loss? What's up with that? I don't have memory loss. At least I don't think I do. There are a lot of questions with no answers. I'm glad Paige is here with me, she has made this more bearable and it would be much more frightening if I were alone. She's funny too. She makes me laugh. She can come up with the funniest stuff. She's fearless, isn't she? Not me though, oh no. I jump at my own shadow. I hope we don't lose our friendship when we get back home. Paige and I. What do you think Joy?"

Joy pushed closer to Ashley.

"I'd like to take you home with me Joy girl, but I don't know when I'll get home, or even if I'll get home. And then there is this mystery surrounding the Seven Seals of Heaven. Why in the world would God allow two silly teenage girls to be responsible for finding such treasure? And tell me Joy. Do I inspire such confidence in you? I think not. And how do you suppose someone got into Heaven, under God's nose, if you would, to steal the Seven Seals anyway. That's probably the greatest mystery of all right there. And then there is Michael. Girl, if you had seen him you would know exactly what I'm talking about. He is ferocious looking. He is big, bigger than anyone I've ever seen. Why Joy, he is bigger than Mr. Clean with hair. He sure has a sense of humor too. Paige was saying some pretty off the wall stuff and Michael laughed so hard. He laughs like my Mom, you know, spontaneously. When something is funny you laugh. It's the best medicine known to man. That's what my Mom says anyway, and she would know because she's a nurse. We had a cookout one summer and all my Mom's friends came from the hospital where she works. I never laughed so hard in my life. Her friend Timmy used to work with my Mom on an ambulance and they had such funny stories to tell. They had everyone laughing too. It was great seeing my Mom happy for a change."

A single tear rolled down Ashley's face and dropped off her chin.

"I miss her. She is probably worried to death about what has happened to me. Do you suppose time at home and time here is the same? My Nana always said a minute in Heaven is forever in our time. So, when we get home do you think my Mom will be old or dead? Joy, I want to go home. I really don't know how to find lost things. When I was about eleven or twelve, I lost one of my new shoes that my Mom had bought me for Easter. I looked everywhere for that shoe and I hadn't been many places so it didn't take me that long to look but I never found it. I really liked those shoes too. I'm pretty sure I won't be able to find God's Seals either. I guess what I'm saying, Joy girl, is, that I'm simply a teenager. I could be anyone you know. I am nobody special, certainly no one with any special talents. Just your average girl with average talents and compared to some kids, I live an okay life. So, why pick me? Why pick Paige? She can't remember what kind of life she has at home or where home is for that matter. I'm telling you Joy girl, there is more mystery here than on <u>Murder She Wrote</u>."

A soft snoring sound came from Joy's nose. The sound was comforting somehow. Ashley smiled and continued to rub Joy's head and talk.

"I hope my brothers don't go in my room and bother my things. They are always wanting my computer games and music and such, and please don't leave any money lying around. They do the loot found in international waters thing. You know, finders, keepers. They are eleven and twelve. They're cute but pesky. They will grow out of that someday. My younger sister doesn't really bother my things as much as she likes to talk. I don't know where she got that, do you Joy? She is always asking me for advice. Like who am I to give advice huh? She doesn't always get along with Mom either. She and Mom are more alike in looks and temperament, so when they argue it gets pretty heated. Me, I guess I'm more like my Dad, quiet and moody. I used to not say anything about the stuff my Mom said or did but as I've gotten older and I guess braver, I have spoken my mind. Not that it's done any good. The gap between Mom and me has been growing wider for a while now. It's like we're not even on the same page. She doesn't understand me and I certainly don't understand her. Nana says there is always going to be a gap between believers and unbelievers. Although my Nana says my Mom is a believer that has just lost her way. I remember seeing a sign out in front of this church once. It said Jesus made a bridge to God with two boards and three nails. I made the comment that I thought the bridge was really made with Jesus' broken body. My Mom asked me why I had to be so legalistic all the time. All I could think of was what Jesus suffered for me and felt like crying. Battered and broken. That's how I feel sometimes after trying to talk to my Mom about Jesus. Like I've been beaten verbally, you know? There has to be a way to reach her Joy. Mom says I'm not very sensitive or kind when it comes to her. I try to be but I get so mad that she can live the way she does without thought or regret in how her life choices affect her children. She says she is happy. Happy? Her happiness is built on a lie. One big lie the devil told her."

A coldness went through Ashley and left her chilled.

"Joy, we need to get back to the fire. It's getting cold and David will surely be wondering where you have got off too."

As Ashley was lifting Joy, preparing to rise from the rock she was sitting on, David walked through the fog. When he saw Joy in Ashley's arms he exclaimed.

"Joy! Is she hurt?"

Reaching to take her from Ashley, Ashley replied.

"No, just asleep. She followed me to this rock and I've been talking to her. She fell asleep. I was probably pretty boring for a little lamb. She kept me company while I told her the story of my young life. She is wonderful David. You must love her very much."

"I love all my sheep."

Ashley patted Joy's head snuggled into David's arms.

"She must trust you a lot to feel so protected."

David's beautiful eyes became serious as he looked into Ashley's eyes.

"There are many things wild on a mountain. Deadly things. Things sheep can't protect themselves from. I am the shepherd. I protect my sheep. To my sheep I am all sufficient. I take care of all their needs. Now come, we must get settled for the night. We have a long day ahead of us tomorrow."

David led the way back to the fire. Ashley found Paige on the mat David had placed on the ground for them, curled on her side, wrapped in a blanket by the fire, sound asleep. Snuggling next to Paige, Ashley was soon asleep too. Only David remained awake. Asking the Lord for protection through the night for himself and his sheep he added the girls saying.

"O continue Thy lovingkindness to those who know Thee, and Thy righteousness to the upright in heart. Let these strangers rest in You and wait patiently for You. Help me to know how to help these whom You have sent me this day. I will guard my eyes and my ways O Lord, my salvation. Hear my prayer Lord. I am Your servant always."

The sheep were suddenly restless. David's sharp eyes checked the perimeter of his camp. Looking into the darkness he felt his sheep's restlessness in his own spirit. Tossing a large piece of wood into the fire he said.

"You feel the evil here too don't you sheep? Is it the strangers? I think not, more likely something seeking the strangers."

Taking up his sword and his shield, David crossed his arms over his chest and leaned his broad shoulders back onto the rock and went to sleep.

Chapter 9

Morning came early for the girls. They just had time to run to the bushes before David started moving his sheep.

"Good thing we have this bag of food. A person could starve to death around here."

Sleeping on the ground and getting up early did nothing to improve Paige's mood.

Ignoring her, Ashley turned to see where David was.

He was bending over a very large sheep looking at one of her back feet.

"What's wrong David?"

"Shemmy has a thorn stuck in the pad of her foot. I am having trouble pulling it out."

Paige walked over and looked at the foot.

"Do you want me to try? I can use my fingernails to grip the thorn."

"Yes, that would be most kind of you. Thorns work their way deeper into the foot if not removed soon enough. I did not notice her limping."

Getting down beside the large sheep Paige looked at the thorn to see which way would be best for her to try and remove it. The sheep's pad was swollen and she could barely see the top of the large thorn.

"It's deep." Paige frowned as she concentrated on the thorn.

"Yes. If you cannot remove the thorn I will have to cut it out. It will be most painful for Shemmy but the thorn has to come out."

Ashley is now looking over Paige's shoulder.

"You better jerk it out quickly, that sheep is getting restless. The others too."

With David holding the sheep's foot in a tight grip, Paige secures her nails around the end of the thorn and pulls hard. The sheep utters a loud bawling sound and kicks her foot knocking Paige flat on the ground. Smiling she holds up the thorn.

"Got it!"

"Yeah and the sheep got you. Your chin and lip are bleeding." Ashley helps Paige to her feet.

"Oh, is it bad?" Paige wipes blood from her chin.

"Nope, just a scratch, but you're gonna have a bruise. What is David doing?"

Both girls watch as David puts a salve on the sheep's pad and wraps the foot in a rag torn from a bigger piece of material.

"Why go to all that trouble? It's just a sheep. The thing will likely step on something else and how long do you think that rag will stay on her foot?" Paige looked at David curiously.

"Her name is Shemmy and I always take care of her this way as well as the others. It's the merciful thing to do. I am the shepherd. My sheep depend on me for everything. Who do you depend on Paige?"

"Me? I don't know. I guess I depend on myself. I'm pretty independent. I can't remember if I've always been like that but it feels right. How about you Ashley?"

"My Mom and Nana have always looked out for us. Both are nurses and taking care of people comes natural for them. I liked that they took care of us but I always made a big deal about being able to take care of myself. I always thought of myself as responsible. I guess in that sense you and I are alike. Paige, we can look out for each other until we get home. Sound good?"

"Yeah, I guess. I need to wash my hands."

They both used the dew on a bush to wet their hands. Rubbing her hands together Paige said.

"Where is the sanitizer when you need it?"

She and Ashley laughed when David looked puzzled.

"Don't ask."

"No, I will not. We must get going. The next green pasture is a fair trip up the mountain."

Shepherding sheep up unidentified paths on a mountain was no easy task. Stubborn sheep would try to wander off, some would get behind because they couldn't stop eating the green grass that grew in patches here and there. Others tried to pick fights with the smaller sheep, and David kept them all in line with a kind word here, a sharp word there and with the occasional yank on the neck with his shepherd's staff. Watching him interact with his sheep fascinated Ashley and Paige both. He had a gentleness about him that was unmistakable. The sheep recognized this and followed him. The girls recognized it as well and followed him too. There was something else about David that each girl recognized. He was very humble and meek. Qualities not often found in the teenage boys they were familiar with.

As Ashley and Paige walked, Paige took the opportunity to ask Ashley questions that had started rolling around in her head.

"Ashley, why do you suppose Michael sent us to this mountain? Do you think David has the Seal?"

Ashley looked up the path they were following to watch David pull a lamb out of some bushes. The smile on his face was beautiful as he patted the lamb and continued to walk.

"No, I don't believe he has the Seal. I'm not sure why we are here. Maybe the Seal is on the mountain somewhere. Maybe there is something David knows that we can use to find the Seal. Honestly, I don't know anymore than you know. I can't think of any reason for being here and I can't believe God really thinks we are capable of finding anything here except blistered feet and dirt. I am no Nancy Drew. What do you think?"

"Me? I can't even remember where I live or how I got involved in this escapade to begin with. I don't believe any of this is real anyway. I'm just here for the food. Sherlock Holmes I am not."

Both girls laughed, and then Paige asked about David.

"What's so special about David?"

"Contrary to popular belief, I am not an expert on the Bible. I know the most common stories about David that are taught in Sunday school and I saw the movie "David and Bathsheba". I know that David became King when he was thirty years old and that he was a great King. He became fascinated with Bathsheba when he saw her bathing and his relationship with her caused great trouble and heartache for David. David and Bathsheba had a son that died because of David's sin and later Solomon was born to them. Solomon was the wise King. David was a good and kind shepherd and that wisdom made him a great King. He was the apple of God's eye.

We could certainly learn from David. I just don't know what it is that God wants us to learn or how that knowledge can help us find the Seal."

"Wow! That's interesting. Too bad we can't educate David to future trouble."

"Absolutely not! Please don't say anything about his future. David is the line from which Jesus comes from. Michael trusts us to not say anything. We are here to learn and find the lost Seals. We are not here to change the future. Agreed?"

"Of course. I wouldn't dream of saying anything. I don't know anything anyway. Like I said, I'm just here for the food."

"You are so funny. David is very good with the sheep, don't you think?"

"Oh yeah. He smells like the sheep too."

"Yeah, I'll bet we smell like that by tonight."

Both girls look down at the sheep around their legs and laughed.

Chapter 10

Following David and his sheep up the mountain allowed both girls time to think about David's goodness. His strength of character. The quality of being good.

Ashley, who was behind Paige asked the question that had been on her mind all day.

"I know David doesn't have the Seal, so where do you suppose the Seal is? Do you think where it is, has anything to do with David?"

"I was wondering the same thing. Do you think we need to go through that big old knapsack he carries around? Surely, the Seal wouldn't be in there. I know, David doesn't have it. Do you think the Seal is somewhere on the mountain? If it is I can't imagine where. Oh, my goodness, these sheep really stink!"

"Yes, they really do." Ashley laughs at Paige trying to not step in sheep poo.

"I have no sense of time here. No timeline for events to happen. David said he was seventeen, our age and I think that's how old he was when he killed Goliath. It seems like he was anointed by Samuel first though. I wish I knew my Bible better."

"Ashley please… you are about to make me lose my humanity and cause me to howl at the moon. If you would just stop and think, you would know without a doubt that we couldn't possibly be in Bethlehem. We are either dreaming or we are dead. No one, but no one can go back in time and you are talking about Bible history. For crying out loud! Be realistic about this, will ya?

Would you look at that sheep! She can't even walk without leaving evidence of her passage on the ground. The smell is enough to permanently remove any appetite anyone ever thought to have. Not to mention, it burns the hair right out of your nose. Ugh! Boy it's hot."

Paige jumped back and forth with her thoughts, unable to settle on any one subject for long.

"First of all, Paige, you can't howl at the moon because it's daytime and second of all whose dream are we in yours or mine. I don't know how we are in Bethlehem but we are and last but not least Wiggles is amazing. How can anyone not get tired just watching her walk. I hope we stop soon, my feet are killing me and I think I have picked up some travelers because I'm itching all over."

David came walking over to them with a small lamb draped over his shoulders. When the girls looked at him in question he said.

"He was tired. Giving him time to rest. We are almost there. We will camp for tonight and finish the trip tomorrow. There is a natural water fall near where we're camping if you want to wash up and all. I'll wash up after you both are done. Not that I smell or anything. Hey, not that you two, smell bad either."

He walked back to the head of the sheep laughing at the disbelieving looks on both their faces.

"Did he just say we stink?" Paige looked at Ashley and then winced as she got a whiff of body odor.

"I hope that smell is coming from you and not me."

"Don't hold your breath sister. I think we both stink. Do you think he has soap?"

Their laughter could be heard on the wind as they followed the sheep to their stopping point.

Chapter 11

The camp was setup in a natural looking corral made from rocks that had fallen from the rock face. Walking around the side of the mountain the waterfall could be heard. There was a small pool that the water fell into from the side of the mountain. Perfect for bathing.

"Once we settle the sheep and get a fire going you can come here and clean up."

David lead the way back around to the sheep. There was already a small pit from previous fires. He started picking up fallen limbs and dead wood laying on the ground.

"We have to have enough wood to keep the fire going all night. Lions roam the mountain at night looking for their next meal. They will be attracted by the smell of the sheep. The fire will discourage the bravest of lions from attacking. Once we settle for the night no one should venture out of camp. It's for your safety and ours."

Ashley and Paige nodded their heads in understanding. Neither wanted to be lion food. They busied themselves picking up wood and stacking them in David's pile.

Once the sheep were settled and the fire was going strong Ashley looked over at Paige to see if she was ready to go to the waterfall. Paige nodded at her and they both looked at David.

"Uhh, David, do you by any chance have any soap with you?" Ashley seemed embarrassed to ask.

"Soap?"

"Yes, you know, a bar of soap to get the dirt off with."

"Oh, you mean cleaning salts." David reached in his knapsack and pulled a large bar of what looked to be mud.

"This is from the dead sea. It cleans the skin very good. When you are done, just leave it on the large rock by the water. I will find it. I made you a torch to take with you. There is a hole in the same rock to hold the torch. Don't wander off from the waterfall please. Yell if you need help."

Both girls nodded and assured David that they would not wander pass the water. Grabbing the mud cake and the flaming torch they made their way to the waterfall.

"This is heavenly isn't it Ashley. The water is just warm enough to make it tolerable. I had no idea a bath could be this amazing." Paige ducked her head under the water before reaching for the mud cake.

"Yeah and that soap is great. I had no idea when he pulled that thing out of his bag that it would lather so much. I don't think I have ever been this clean before. Did it burn your skin? It burned my skin a little when I first started using it."

"Yeah I think it's the salt. We are not used to using salt soap from the dead sea. You know you can buy this stuff everywhere at home. I'm going to start using it when I get home. Home."

Paige looked at Ashley and straight on asked.

"Are we ever going to get home Ashley? We have to wake up sometime because if we don't then we have to be dead and this is some afterlife adventure. I'm glad I'm with you but for goodness sake somebody has got to be missing me. Unless I can't remember things because I never existed. Maybe you're dead and I'm your guide to whatever."

"No, you aren't my guide because you don't know where we are either. You are just as lost as me. We can't be in a dream because we don't know who is dreaming me or you. And I refuse to believe I'm dead. A touch of cold mist hit Ashley's face. A feeling of evil touched her mind and suddenly Ashley felt fear. Let's get out of this water. I'm cold and I'm looking like a prune. This place feels creepy."

They left everything where David said to. Paige's hair was short so she had no trouble shaking the water out of it. Ashley's hair was long, practically below her rear end and it took a little time to squeeze the water out before she could pull it back and secure it with the tie that managed to travel back with her. After they dressed they walked back around the mountain to the fire. David had their blankets ready for them and reminding them to stay by the fire he goes to the waterfall for his bath.

Eating from the bag of manna Paige once again starts talking about being in a dream.

"Paige! Stop! We are not dreaming!" Ashley is beginning to get upset.

"Oh, come on Ashley. Bethlehem is Bible history. We did not go back in time. It is an impossibility. Walking in a dream world or walking in a dead world. Of Course, if David had been real he would of course be dead now. So where do you think that leaves us." Paige crossed her arms over her chest and adopted a smug look.

Ashley jumped to her feet and started toward the fog.

"Ashley! David said don't leave the fire."

"I'm not going far, just to the little girl's bush."

And she was gone.

Chapter 12

Ashley walked into the fog without looking back. Her mind was flooded with thoughts, chaotic, fragmented thoughts. Tears dripped from eyes not focused on anything. Her feet moved her forward automatically. Her main object was to walk until she was exhausted, hoping the exhaustion would calm her raging thoughts and bring peace to her mind. Who was she kidding, Paige was right all along. The shepherd boy David's Bethlehem was Bible history. Were they dreaming? Was any of this real?

"Am I dead Lord?"

With that question, the bottom of her world fell out. Tears flooded her cheeks and into the night Ashley screamed.

"Mom! Mom, where are you? I'm so scared Mom. Can you hear me?"

Ashley felt a brush of cold. It felt like a touch of evil and stumbling she looked wildly around her for the source of her discomfort. Looking back through the fog Ashley suddenly realized that she couldn't see the reflection of the fire or hear the sheep's bells or bleats. How far from Paige and David had she gotten? Then she remembered David talking about lions being on the mountain. Fear nearly paralyzed her.

"Paige? David?" The fear made her voice tremble.

Cold brushed around her again.

Ashley's thoughts cascaded through her mind in a scrambled fashion and she began to cry in earnest. Turning around in a circle she had no idea in which direction she came from or which direction she needed to go in to return to the safety of the fire and Paige and David.

Cold pushed at her mind.

"Hello? Is somebody there? Paige? David?"

True fear filled her mind and pushed everything else out. Ashley suddenly realized she was not alone and that she was in danger. Which direction should she go in? Ashley hesitated and then.

Something warm and soft rubbed against her leg. She screamed and through her scream she heard the soft bleat of a lamb. Not just any lamb. Joy.

"Joy! Oh Joy. You sweet, wonderful lamb. Which direction did you come from?"

Bending down Ashley picked the lamb up and pushed her tear stained face into the wool that was Joy. Just hearing the bleat of the little lamb made her feel not quite so alone.

Holding the lamb in close to her chest Ashley again felt the brush of cold almost running through her. Her heartbeat picked up and with a voice that trembled with fear Ashley said again.

"Hello?"

Cold brushed against her again and with the cold came a sound that pushed at her mind. Frowning, Ashley backed up and fell over a rock. She lost her grip on the lamb and Joy fell out of her arms. Bleating with alarm Joy bounded away. Ashley couldn't see which direction Joy went in and true terror ran through her.

"Joy! Come back Joy! Please don't leave me here all alone. Joy! I'm so scared! Joy?"

Tears of terror almost froze on her face as Ashley got to her feet.

From somewhere in the fog came a roaring sound.

"Joy."

Cold pushed against her again and it came.

A growl, not loud but near.

"Who's there? Paige? David? Please, say something, you're scaring me to death!"

Another growl, and something warm hit her face, a breath.

"Joy?"

"I'm coming for you. Run! Run!"

Pure evil pushed at Ashley's thoughts.

Instinct took over a mind in overload and Ashley began to run.

"Faster!"

Rocks, tree branches, thorn bushes all made themselves known to the girl as she literally ran on winged feet from the danger that sought her life. Wet grass made her fall but she was up in a flash running for all she was worth.

"That's it, run. You're all alone. No one knows where you are or cares. Your mother wished a thousand times that you had not been born. You made her life miserable. Run, relief is waiting for you. This is all just a bad dream. You will wake and find yourself in your bed with another boring day ahead of you."

The oily, smooth voice purred in her head. The sound was unlike anything Ashley had ever heard before and hoped to never hear again. It was everywhere but nowhere all at the same time. The sound filled her heart with dread and scattered her thoughts like ice cubes from an overflowing ice machine.

"Don't slow down now, you're almost there. Comfort is waiting for you. You deserve to die but you'll live. I can taste your fear. I hear your heart beating in your puny little chest."

Irrational laughter filled her head. In all of Ashley's seventeen years she had never been exposed to such evil. The voice dripped pure evil. Like icing on a cupcake left in the microwave too long. Nervous laughter bubbled up inside her but fear kept it at bay.

Running, Ashley tried to pull her terrified thoughts together but was unable to think beyond her next foot step.

Fog closed her in a wet cocoon.

"Mom, forgive me, I didn't mean to make your life miserable."

Ashley now could not tell the difference between the wet fog and her tears, and she was so cold, so very cold. Missing her step Ashley fell. Panic made her crawl on hands and knees until she was able to get on her feet again.

"Oh, isn't that sweet? Mom forgive me. She can't hear you little girl. Run, you, miserable little snit!" The voice rolled over Ashley like a serpent.

Ashley's feet fairly flew over the ground in her effort to get away from that voice. Her thoughts were chaotic but somehow Ashley latched onto her Grandmother's voice.

"Put your eyes on Jesus."

"Lord, You Lord, You said, You would help me. Please help me!" The cry came from her soul.

In a hospital room far away, blue eyes as deep as the sea suddenly blazed with a fierce light.

Arms stretched with a mighty wing span to envelope the small girl in the hospital bed.

"Yes Father!" Was spoken in a voice soft as cotton but with the strength of steel.

"Stop!"

Ashley skidded to a stop. Suddenly the ground beneath her feet began to give way. Sensing nothing but empty space in front of her, Ashley looked to her left for something to break her fall into nothingness. The tree loomed small but sturdy beside her. Grabbing on to the extending branch, Ashley held on for all she was worth.

"No!!!! Nothing but comfort awaits you child. Turn the branch loose and let yourself find release. You are dreaming and will wake soon. Paige is right, there is no God. There is only peace in death. Trust me, you cannot trust your God to save you."

The evil voice was sing song oily. A bone, weary wash of ice cold nothing hit Ashley in an effort to break her hold on the tree.

"Jesus!"

Again and again Ashley was hit with cold washes of nothing. She was tired, cold, filled with an unnamed fear and losing her tight hold on the tree. The thought filtered through her mind that maybe it would be easier for her and all concerned if she just let go. Maybe it was all just a dream and she would wake up and find herself at home in bed facing another boring day.

"I love You Lord."

It was a weak whisper but it was heard.

"Put on your armor!"

"Armor? What armor?" Ashley's face frowned as she tried to think.

"As in 'be strong in the Lord, and in the strength of His might'? I memorized that when I was little. How does it go now? 'Put on the full armor of God, that you may be able to stand firm against the schemes of the devil. For our struggle is not against flesh and blood, but against the rulers, against the powers, against the world forces of this darkness, against the spiritual forces of wickedness in the heavenly places. Therefore, take up the full armor of God, that you may be able to resist in the evil day, and having done everything, to stand firm. Stand firm therefore, having girded your loins with truth, and having put on the breastplate of righteousness, and having shod your feet with the preparation of the gospel of peace; in addition to all, taking up the shield of faith with which you will be able to extinguish all the flaming missiles of the evil one. And take the helmet of salvation, and the sword of the spirit, which is the word of God.'

After the first five words from the scripture of Ephesians 6:10-17, Ashley's voice became strong in her quotation. Never doubting her memory and thanking her Sunday School Teacher, Mrs. Ashe, for making her learn scripture verses, Ashley realized there was utter silence around her. Was the voice gone? Was she safe? Was he the devil? No. She never saw anyone. She just felt a presence. A shadow of a presence. A shadow of evil.

Finding a firm place to plant her foot, Ashley worked her sore body around the little tree that she still had a death grip on, to finally find firm ground. Hesitant to completely turn loose of the last limb, and on her hands and knees, Ashley crawled away from the cliff's edge.

"Thank you for saving me Lord. Now, can you point me in the general direction of Paige, David, his smelly sheep and that glorious fire? Please let Joy be okay."

Ashley started walking back in the direction of David's camp. How she knew it was the right direction she couldn't say, she just knew.

Ashley heard the sheep before she saw the glow of the fire. What she saw when she entered the camp caused her to stop dead still.

"He's been like this ever since Joy came running into camp." Paige was sitting with her back against a rock, rubbing Joy's wooly body.

David was on his knees praying.

"David?"

David raised his head to look at Ashley.

"The evil one was on the mountain tonight."

"The evil one?" Cold chills ran up and down her body.

"Yes."

Understanding lite a fire in Ashley's eyes.

Joy bleated as Paige jumped up and faced Ashley and David.

"Come on! Give me a break would you please. You both are breaking my heart with this stuff. The evil one was on the mountain? What are you talking about? You know what I think? I think when we got dumped on this mountain you fell on your head. I'm going for a walk."

"Paige? Look at me. Please? What do you see?"

Ashley held onto Paige's arm pleading with her with her eyes.

"I see you. Of course, you are a little messed up. Actually, a lot messed up. Bloody too. Why are you bloody? Ashley? Are you alright?"

It became the most important thing in her life at that moment to put her arms around Paige and hold on. Sobs tore at her and made it difficult for Paige to hear her.

"It followed me and I almost fell off the mountain. You should have seen it, heard it."

"What was it? What did you see?"

David grabbed his shield and sword.

"Was it in the shape of a lion or bear? I will check the camp. My sheep have not sensed anything but lions and bears can grab sheep fast and run with them."

Before Ashley could say anything, David stepped into the fog and disappeared from sight.

Paige twisted her ring around and around on her finger with her left hand as she looked into Ashley's blue eyes. Eyes that were opened wide with shock.

"I saw, I felt, I had the feeling of evil."

Ashley looked back in the direction she had come from.

Paige shook her as she exclaimed more forcefully.

"But what did you see?"

"It was just as shadow."

Ashley felt helpless as she looked at Paige.

"You saw a shadow? A shadow of evil?"

This was said incredulously.

"Yes, yes that was it. The shadow of evil. It spoke to me." Tearful eyes looked at Paige.

"A shadow spoke to you?"

"Yes. It said my mom did not want me, that I made her miserable. That everyone would be better off if I were dead. That you were right,

48

we were dreaming and that there is no God to save me. I was running and if Michael had not said Stop I would have run off the mountain into nothing."

"Michael said stop?"

"Yes, and he told me to put on my armor."

"Really? Is that how you got so banged up? Running through the bushes and all? And what armor? Ashley you don't have armor. Are you all right?"

"Yes." Ashley felt as if she had just run a six mile race, and won. Thinking fast, Ashley tries to explain to Paige what she felt.

"Don't you get it Paige? What was it David said? 'Yea though I walk through the valley of the shadow of death….'"

"Death you dummy not evil."

Paige abruptly let go of Ashley and turned to look at the fire as it crackled and sent up little fireflies as if in warning of something coming.

"Yes Paige, he said death, but there would not be death if it were not for evil. I felt the shadow of evil. David even said that the evil one was on the mountain tonight."

"Yeah, and he also said 'I will fear no evil…?'"

"Yes, he did, but you or David did not see, hear, or feel this, this…"

Ashley looked lost and a little shocked again. Tears fell from her eyes.

"Paige, it was more frightening than any sensation I have ever had and for the first time in my life I wanted my Father."

"But I thought you said…"

Paige looked at Ashley with a puzzled look on her face as Ashley interrupted her with…

"My Heavenly Father, Paige."

"There you go again. You know I don't believe that stuff. Just as your Dad hasn't been there neither has God. God doesn't exist. But listen, right now it doesn't matter. Your face is bleeding.

Paige reached out and gently touched Ashley's face.

"Please be careful Ashley, I may act fearless but I'm not. I would have no idea what to do, where to go or how to get there without you."

Ashley laughed at her.

"I hit a tree branch that was as hard as your head.

They both laughed as Paige said.

49

"But did you go to the little girl's bush?"

"No, that thing scared the need right out of me."

Paige grabbed Ashley's hand and headed off in another direction saying.

"Come on, I've got to go too. Let's go while David is tending to the needs of his sheep. For safety's sake, we'll go together. That shadow better not mess with me. I'm about to explode."

Laughing but looking behind her, Ashley followed Paige into the bushes.

Chapter 13

Morning dawned bright and early once again. The day was clear as if the fog had never been. Everything looked different in the day. The terror of the night was gone, replaced with sunshine and moving sheep. David's little band of sheep herders were headed with him further up the mountain. The walking was slow as they each had to occasionally head off a lamb or sheep that was determined to go astray. Either girl could not figure out how David kept these sheep in line by himself because they were constantly running after them. When they mentioned to him how he couldn't possibly watch these sheep by himself he would just grin and keep walking.

"So, he thinks he has a secret method of shepherding sheep. Surely it can't be that difficult."

"Who cares Ashley. You are so competitive. Look at that sheep. When he walks his rump nearly hits his middle. He walks with a wriggle. I see why David named him Wiggles. He's so cute! I believe he likes me. Watch out Wiggles, you are going to make me fall. Oh Ashley, I want to take him home with me."

Ashley laughs as she watches Wriggles and Paige play as they follow David to the high pasture.

They reach a flat area on the mountain where David stops for lunch and a rest. After eating from their bag of manna, Paige looks over Ashley's shoulder and sees one of the sheep running toward the meadow.

"Oh snap! That sheep finally managed to get away. Help me round her up will you Ashley?"

The girls take off after the sheep as David yells that he will set up camp.

"Which way do you think that sheep went?"

Paige looked in every direction.

"Well, there is a print in the ground over here by this bush. Does it look like a sheep print?"

Ashley was bent at the waist looking down at the ground.

"Well, I don't know my dear Watson. What does a sheep print look like?"

Paige was barely holding back her laughter.

"I'm not sure. Do they have two pads or three?"

"You should know Paige, you pulled that thorn out of that sheep's foot."

"Shemmy. I removed a thorn from Shemmy's foot and I got a busted lip to prove it. She had two pads."

"Then we're in luck. This print has two indentions"

"We go this way."

Ashley took off after Paige through the bushes.

"Good job Watson. Lead the way."

Paige laughed as she pushed through the bushes with Ashley.

"Bubbles? Bubbles? Where are you? Who names their sheep Bubbles?"

Ashley blew her bangs out of her eyes with a puff and leans against a tree to rest.

"David would. He said the sheep would have bubbles around her mouth when she was a baby and was nursing. David said she was a greedy little thing. The real question is how does he tell one sheep from another. They kinda all look the same."

"Yeah. We better get moving. At this rate, we won't find anything."

Both girls started moving through the bushes and tall grass.

"Hey. I found another print."

Ashley stopped to take a closer look at the ground.

"Ugh, Paige. Something doesn't look right about this print."

"Duh Sherlock! That's because it's bigger, has four toes and a pad. The toes have points. Like claws. It looks like a tiger."

Paige shuddered.

"Mountains don't have tigers. But they do have."

"Mountain lions!" They both said together.

"We need a weapon Paige."

Ashley looked around.

"All I see is bushes, meadow flowers and butterflies."

"Yeah. Where is David with his sword when you need him?"

"Who needs David when you have this?"

Ashley holds up a long, large limb from the tall grass growing beside a bush next to a rock.

"Good job. Let's go find that sheep. I'll be right behind you."

Paige looks around cautiously.

The girls spread out a little and begin calling the sheep again.

A slight noise stops Paige in her tracks.

"Ashley, did you hear that?"

"Yeah. Which direction did it come from? Bubbles?"

"Baa, baa."

"This way Ashley."

Paige took off through the tall grass.

"Paige! Slow down. There could be."

Paige's scream chilled the blood in Ashley's veins.

Looking around Ashley couldn't see Paige anywhere.

"Paige! Where are you? Answer me Paige! I can't find you."

"Stop Ashley! Don't take another step."

"Paige, I hear you but I can't see you. Where are you?"

"Down here."

"Where?"

"Down here. Get on your knees and crawl forward but be careful. I'm in a hole."

Ashley drops to her knees and starts crawling.

"Stop Ashley. I'm down here."

"Baa."

"Oh, sorry. Bubbles is down here too. If she weren't I'd have had a rougher landing."

"I see you both. Ha Ha. You guys come on out. We need to get back to David. No telling what or who is out here with us."

"Well then Rapunzel. Just let down your hair."

"Oh. Sorry. Let's see. Bubbles first I guess. Can you lift her up for me to grab?"

"I think so. Let's try. She had better have complete bladder control, not to mention bowel control."

Grunting and lots of laughter, Paige finally pushes the sheep up enough for Ashley to grab her. Ashley hauls her up falling on her back with Bubbles on top.

"Ugh, Bubbles. You have very bad breath darling. Crest would do wonders for you."

"Ok, ok. Enough. Get me out of here already."

"Sorry Paige. Bubbles and I were doing the bonding thing. I'm going to hold my stick down to you. Do you think you could use it to crawl out?"

"I can try. Let's give it a go dearie."

After two splinters for Ashley and three for Paige plus wild laughter, Paige finally was able to crawl out of the hole.

"Ashley, you remember that scene in The Wizard of Oz where they are rescuing Dorothy? The lion is climbing up the mountain and the others are holding onto his tail, hoping his tail doesn't fall off? That's exactly what I was thinking while holding onto your stick crawling out of that hole."

They both started laughing at the thought of the lion's tail falling off.

Ashley, Paige and Bubbles made their way back to David's camp.

While Ashley is telling David about their adventure, Paige looks over and sees wild flowers growing next to a large rock. She wanders over toward the rock, with intentions to pick flowers. As she gets closer to the flowers her mouth drops open and she gasps with delight. Hundreds of different flowers are everywhere. She begins picking flowers and humming to herself. With her arms full of beautiful flowers, she looks up at the cloudless blue sky. She wonders how far up she is on the mountain and how close to the sky she must be.

"I am on a mountain, as far from home as forever is, on a mission for God with a girl I did not know only days ago... helped by a shepherd boy from a Bible story from thousands of years ago. Does anybody but me find this absolutely ridiculous? Send me straight to the looney bin right now. Ashley is wrong! This has to be a dream. I'm on a mission for God? And you know, God has been suspiciously silent in all of this, He's not real. Am I dead? Mom, where are you? I am so scared that I won't be able to help Ashley find the Seals and I won't get the chance to find out where I belong and who I belong to. God, are You real? I know no one can hear me. Please, whatever this is, where ever I am, please let my family know that I'm here and I love them."

Tears of complete heartbreak fall from Paige's blue eyes as she looks up at an equally blue sky. "I have to leave this with you. Trust you to make this all right."

A light wind blows through the tall grass as birds fly from branch to branch, as butterflies move from flower to flower, all as if the Lord is saying 'I've got this, you can trust me.'

With a lighter heart Paige turns from the meadow to go back to her friends when she comes face to face with the largest cat she has ever seen.

Instinct makes her go completely still. A hysterical giggle nearly breaks from her mouth as she wonders why she was never taught what to do when facing a lion large enough to swallow her whole.

Both Paige and the lion are startled when out of nowhere a large fat sheep comes flying through the tall grass and jumps on the lion's back.

With a roar, the lion is all over the sheep and Paige is flying through the grass on feet that barely touch the ground.

"David! Help!"

The roars and growls of the lion and the bleating cries of the sheep are loud on the otherwise quiet mountain breeze.

Complete shock causes Paige's feet to grow wings and she is almost flattened to the ground by David's sudden appearance in her path to safety.

"A lion!"

David rushes past her with his sword and shield and a cry worthy of a true warrior bursting through the roars of the lion.

The coppery smell of blood makes Paige's stomach roll and as Ashley reaches her Paige vomits the contents of her stomach into a bush.

"Paige! Are you alright? Is that a lion? Oh, my goodness! That is a lion."

With the shout of righteousness, David slays the lion.

David backs away from the dead lion and sits on the grass. He has three long scratches down his right arm, with blood running down his tunic sleeve.

Paige slowly walks up to him unable to tear her eyes from the bloody mass that was Wiggles lying in the grass beside David.

"Wiggles! Oh, Wiggles. Why did it have to be you? Why did you have to die?" Paige drops to her knees beside David, sobbing.

"To save you. He jumped on the lion to save you." Ashley turned tear drenched eyes to David's bowed head.

"I'm sorry, so very sorry David. He saved Paige from the lion. He was trying to protect her."

Paige got to her feet and turned away.

"I wish I had never come to this mountain. I hate smelly sheep!"

"David, are you okay? Your arm is bleeding. Can I look at it? We need to stop the bleeding. My mom's a nurse. I've learned a few things from her. Please, say something."

David gets to his feet and looks at the sheep.

"We have to burn Wiggles. We can't leave him here, he will draw other animals that will be a threat to the other sheep. We will burn the lion also."

Paige walked up to David.

"Oh David, I'm so sorry. This is so horrible, so heartbreaking. I never even knew that he had followed me. There was no one and then there was the lion and then Wiggles came running up and jumped on the lion's back like some caped crusader, and he... and he."

Paige dropped to her knees sobbing.

"I'll get the brush to start the fire."

"I'm so sorry David. I know you have to just hate me now. I loved Wiggles. He made me laugh."

David got to his feet, patted Paige on the back and with one last look at Wiggles he started picking up dry, dead tree branches. He made two separate piles and placed Wiggles on one and then hung the lion between two trees.

"David? What are you doing"

"The lion's hide will make a soft bed. I'm removing the hide before I place the carcass in the fire."

"But David, the lion killed Wiggles. It wanted to kill me. How can you?"

"This is the law of nature Paige. We use what the Lord provides. Yes, the lion killed Wiggles. We all hate that this has happened. But good has come from it. You are safe and we'll have the hide to help keep us warm. Death comes Paige, for us all. But not for you... today. Do you see? Wiggles died so that you would have a chance to live. You had a choice. Stay, fight the lion, maybe save Wiggles but lose your own life, or, let Wiggles do what she came to do. He allowed you to run and find help.

The Lord is our Shepherd Paige, He always provides. The nights have been cold, this hide will help."

With that, David turned back to the lion and began to remove the hide.

Ashley looked up to find Paige watching David. She had a thoughtful expression on her face. Without a word, she walked to David and asked.

"Can I help?"

Together David and Paige removed the hide from the lion and placed it on a rock to dry. Together they hauled the lion's remains to the pile of brush and set it on fire. They placed Wiggles more firmly on the other pile of brush and it too was set on fire.

David kept the sheep close and they all watched both fires long into the night.

The crackling fires prevented the girls from hearing the mourning sounds coming from the sheep for Wiggles.

Chapter 14

Late evening, just as twilight is settling in, Ashley, Paige and David are sitting around the fire, eating manna from Paige's bag. They are laughing at David's stories about events that had happened while caring for his sheep. Ashley recognizes the golden opportunity she now has to really learn about David and his life as the apple of God's eye. This particular story was about Wiggles and his antics.

"You mean he got stuck in a thorn bush?" asked Ashley.

"Stuck? You can say that. A thorn got embedded in the wool on his right hind leg. He didn't get his name for being calm and still. The more he wiggled the more the thorn dug in. And the racket he made, bawling and bleating as loud as he could. I could not hear myself think. It took me forever to get him loose. I had to use my knife to cut the wool from his rear. I cut myself twice during his wiggling about. He would not stay still. When the wool with the thorn in it came loose, he kicked his hind legs, hitting me in the chest, knocking me into the thorn bush. Of course, then, I got a large thorn stuck in my hind quarters. No wool to soften the point of the thorn. He then, wiggle ran, around, as only he could, happy as a lark. I however, limped for two days."

David laughingly rubbed his back side.

Ashley and Paige laughed till tears ran down their cheeks. Then, remembering the lion they all became quiet and thoughtful.

"Wiggles was very brave to sacrifice himself for you Paige. I have never known a sheep to do that before."

David looked at both girls intently.

"Really? He came out of nowhere, never slowing down. He jumped on that lion's back so fast. He shouldn't have done it." Paige whispered.

"If he hadn't done it, you would be dead instead." Ashley touched Paige's head.

"What would I do here in this world without you? I don't know how to take care of sheep. I don't know how to find Seals. I don't know how to get home. I don't even know where home is. Without you, I'm lost and all alone. Heck, I'm lost anyway. There are no seals on this mountain, just smelly sheep and David. Oh, and, lions, tigers and bears… oh my! Okay, it's official, I'm losing it." Ashley laughs and then says.

"But really Paige. The Seals aren't on this mountain."

"Well I think that obvious, don't you?"

"So why did Michael send us here, to the mountain?"

"Maybe he sent us to David."

"David? Do you have any idea why God would send us to find His Seal and have us start here on your mountain with you and your sheep?"

"What I know about God is that in all things He is Sovereign. Through life events He teaches us things we need to know in order to live our lives as His children. He teaches us so we can teach others. Maybe He has something important He wants you both to learn. Both of you or maybe just one of you."

His eyes seek Paige as she draws a breath to refute his statement.

"Before you say anything Paige, just think about it. Even the Evil one knows there is a God. Saying that God isn't real doesn't make it so. God is very real. Look around, all this did not make itself. God created all things and all things were created by Him. Maybe He had to bring you here to teach you this truth. We all stumble. You will too. The truth of that is that when you do, stumble, God is right there to set you right back on your feet. If you stumble enough, maybe, just maybe, you will pick a different path. One that doesn't cause you to stumble. We each choose our own paths in this life. It's the choices we make. To choose to believe or not believe. It's our choice, your choice. Saying God isn't real is only an excuse you make to allow yourself to travel the path you chose. It's not without it's pitfalls by the way. God loves us and He wants the best for us so of course His paths are the better choice but because He allows us to choose, sometimes he has to break us long enough to teach us. I don't know you but I can assure you that God knows everything about you. He made you, why would He not love you. I can also assure you that His best is better than your best any day. Think about what I've said."

"Well that was intense. You have definitely missed your calling."

David looked at Paige with a very puzzled expression,

"You should have been a teacher."

"Somebody has to tend to the sheep."

Ashley was nodding her head when her eyes glanced to David's shield. Taking a deep breath, she says'

"David, your shield is very unique. Will you tell us about it?"

David looks at his shield and smiles.

"Nothing really to say about it. My sword is an old cast off from one of my brothers. It's efficient and gets the job done. I decided a sword needed a shield. Not just any shield though. A shield that the enemy could see coming. God is my Protector, my Shield. I made my physical shield from the olive tree. One night I was looking up at the stars thinking of my Protector when one of the stars caught my eye. It was really bright. Of course, my star on my shield does not shine but truly the enemy will see it coming. It may not be the best drawn star or the prettiest but it works for me."

Ashley smiled as she said.

"Yes. A six, pointed star. The magical power of David's shield. The star of David."

David shook his head.

"No, the shield of David. The Protector of Sheep. God is my Protector, my shield."

"Well, I always wondered about the Star of David. Now I know. It's getting late and I know we will have a big day tomorrow. We need to get a good night's rest."

Realizing Paige had been totally quiet during David's explanation about his shield, Ashley looked at her.

"Paige? Are you ok?"

Concern made Ashley's voice wobble.

"OK? Yes. I just have a lot to think about. Intellectually I guess I can admit I know that there is a God but I don't think He cares about me. And before you say anything Ashley, I really don't care. I have managed to take care of myself for seventeen years now just fine and without any help from above. Don't expect me to jump on the Jesus bandwagon just because a boy who takes care of sheep says the ride is the right choice. I do have to say that I agree with David in that the choice is mine to make. And right now, I choose not to believe. Oh, I believe there is a God, I will give you that, but I don't believe in Him."

"Paige!"

"Not now Ashley. You were right. Tomorrow is another big day. We need sleep. Oh, and David, Trouble has slipped pass you again for greener grass."

David looked in the direction Paige was pointing.

Grabbing the sheep and looking him in the eye David spoke.

"Trouble. You have one more day to misbehave. If you don't stop trying to run away, if you don't start listening and being obedient, I will have to use discipline."

"Discipline? What? Do you spank the sheep?"

Paige laughs at her own joke.

"No. They have to be obedient or they die."

David's voice was very serious.

"Die? Do you kill them?"

Paige was horrified.

"No silly girl. But I do have to teach them to stay with the other sheep. Predators are all around, as you well know Paige. They do not offer second chances."

"Ok. But how do you teach them to not run off?"

"You'll see. I'm afraid Trouble will need a lesson in obedience."

"What I see is Trouble sure earned his name."

Chapter 15

David positioned Ashley ahead of the sheep with himself in the middle and Paige behind him at the end. He kept his eyes on Trouble, never letting her out of his sight. It was easy to see that the young sheep was hard strong and bidding his time to slip off for greener grass.

Her chance came and away she ran.

David was quick and before Trouble knew what got him, David's hand reached out with the crooked end of his shepherd's staff and grabbed his right hind leg and gave a sharp yank.

The young sheep fell to his knees with a loud bellow.

David circled around to face the little sheep and said quietly.

"You must be obedient. Do not run away by yourself. You will get eaten that way."

He then bent to inspect the sheep's right hind leg.

"Broken. Let me brace your leg for the journey to our camp.

The sheep never took his eyes off of David as he quietly cried.

Ashley looked at Paige and raising her hand to Paige's chin, laughingly said.

"Close your mouth Paige. Flies here are mean."

"Mean? What David just did was mean. Why did he purposely break Trouble's leg?"

"To teach him."

"Teach him? Humph!"

"You'll see."

David braced the little sheep's leg and bound it with strips of cloth. He then picked the sheep up and wrapped him around his neck. Picking up his staff he then turned to the girls and said.

"Okay. Let's go. We have a way yet to go before we make camp."

Paige looked surprised and mumbled to herself'

"Just like that? I don't get it. Why break the sheep's leg and then go to the trouble of carrying the thing?"

"The thing's name is Trouble. He needed to learn. Breaking his leg is a reminder. It will heal soon and he will never try to slip off again."

Over the next few days Paige watched David with the little sheep. His gentleness, kindness, and overall goodness was shown over and over again. He stopped to let Trouble eat and drink, and to relieve himself. Then David returned him to his shoulders to travel.

One night while sitting around the fire, Paige watched David bed the little sheep down for the night.

"I don't get it. Why put yourself to so much trouble? First you yell at him. Then you break his leg. Then you set the leg and carry him, not to mention tending to his daily life needs. Looks like it would have been easier to just let the wild animals get him."

"Paige. To learn obedience, it sometimes takes extreme measures. Like breaking his leg. Sure, it was painful for him but not as painful as being eaten alive by a lion. The next time he thinks of running off by himself he will remember the pain and stay with the flock."

"But you carried him, fed him, why?"

"Because he is my sheep. I love him. I want him to know he can trust me to keep him safe."

"But you broke his leg!"

"Yes. To keep him safe."

"Then you carried him around your shoulders for days making sure he had all he needed."

"Paige. It takes very little to show kindness, to be gentle, to be good to someone. Sometimes, in order to do those things, in order for the sheep to slow down long enough for you to do those things, they have to be broken. A little pain now is much better than a lot of pain later or worse, death. Obedience does not come naturally. It is taught. Breaking a leg is a last resort. Trust is also a learned thing. It does not come naturally. You have to understand the difference also of man and beast. For man, breaking a leg is not done to teach him or her obedience. God would use circumstances in their lives to teach. It's easier to teach obedience to children. You know, instruction, consequences for disobedience and so on. But none of us gets too old to learn. It takes courage to live the life God wants you to have. Courage, kindness, gentleness, goodness and many other God given gifts, are freely offered to His children."

Paige grinned.

"Hey, it's like what Cinderella's Mother told her. "Have courage and be kind."

"Cinderella?"

"Never mind."

Paige hid her grin.

As the days went on Paige and Ashley witnessed David's goodness, kindness, and gentleness.

They found themselves following David's example.

Chapter 16

Sitting around the fire, relaxed after another long day of herding sheep, it occurred to Ashley that David had asked them a lot of questions but she had not thought to ask him about his family.

"So, David. You are the youngest of your family?"

"Yes."

"Do you have a close family?"

"Close? Well not very close. Maybe a day's walk. Mostly down the mountain."

"No. Not close in distance. I mean close family as in you all love each other and enjoy being together."

Ashley laughed at herself.

"Love each other? I have never thought of my family and love at the same time. I love my father and brothers. They tolerate me I would say, rather than love me. My father loves me and trusts me to take care of his sheep. He wants and expects the best for us. He worries my brothers will come to harm in the battle with the Philistines. I tell him that God goes before them but he worries none the less."

"Do you wish to be a soldier in Saul's army?"

"I am a shepherd of sheep. My responsibilities are just as important. Besides, I like taking care of my father's sheep. My brothers would not like me being in their way."

David laughed at his own thoughts.

Paige grinned at David as she said.

"You're a good man Charlie Brown."

"Paige! I don't know this Charlie Brown but if you are talking about me... thank you."

Ashley suddenly felt a brush of cold against her skin. The sheep also became a little restless.

"The evil one is on the mountain."

David put more wood on the fire, calmed his sheep with gentle words and picked up his sword and shield. He relaxed with his back against a rock but his eyes were constantly checking the perimeters of camp.

"Girls don't go far from camp to do your necessities and stay together."

"David, you said the evil one is on the mountain. Who is the evil one?"

As Ashley was talking the fog began rolling in.

"Lucifer. God's fallen angel. He seeks to destroy all that God holds dear. God is stronger so do not fear. Sometimes you cannot fight what you do not see. So, it is better to stay out of the way."

"But what if you are the specific target of Lucifer?"

"The Lord is my Shepherd. I shall not fear."

"Before. When I almost fell off the mountain. I believe it was him, trying to cause me harm."

"These Seals that you girls seek. Are they important to God?"

"Yes, and Michael said someone else wants them too, and that someone would harm us to get them."

"The evil one."

"I believe so."

David threw more wood on the fire. Ashley and Paige drew closer to him and the fire.

"The Seals are not on the mountain."

Paige looked at Ashley and then back at David.

"We have come to that conclusion but before we could leave the mountain I had to learn how important kindness, gentleness, and goodness were. I guess you can say lessons of life. No matter what I believe about God and His love, I do believe those three things are important for me to grow as a person and I can't think of a single other person or way in which I could have learned them than from you David. So, thank you."

"As I said Paige, my brothers tolerate me and are somewhat jealous I think. Oh, not of my shepherding skills but I don't know, maybe my relationship with the Lord. I'm not sure. I do know that I will always treat them with goodness, kindness and gentleness. It gets hard sometimes when they are teasing and harsh but I try to stay strong and faithful to my beliefs."

"I will always remember what you just said David and show goodness, kindness and gentleness even when I'd rather not. It does work better."

Suddenly there was the sound of tinkling. As if someone dropped three coins into a bowl.

Everyone heard it but was afraid to mention it in case it was their imagination.

Tears nearly blinded Ashley as she looked at Paige and felt that sisterly proud feeling of accomplishment.

David however felt embarrassed. His already ruddy complexion went a deeper shade of red.

Ashley and Paige laughed at how uncomfortable he was acting.

"Okay. About the Seals. Where do you suppose we look for them, now that we know they are not anywhere, on the mountain.

Paige asked her question but was looking at Ashley. Ashley was thinking how far Paige had come and was not really paying attention.

Ashley smiles as she looks off into the fog. A sound alerts her of someone approaching.

Ashley stiffens. "Do you guys hear that? It sounds like whistling."

Both girls and David looked up and around the enclosure. David jumps up and points to the two large rocks.

"Quick! Hide behind the rocks." He grabs his sword and shield which he had placed at his side.

Dashing behind the rocks, the girls wait quietly. Out of the foggy mist a young boy walks whistling into the sheep camp.

"Jonah!"

David laughs and claps the boy on his back, in the manly man greeting.

"What are you doing here so early?"

David props his sword and shield against the rocks the girls are behind.

"Stay there." he whispers.

"Your father sent me. You are to go into Bethlehem. The Prophet Samuel came to make a sacrifice to the Lord. I guess your father doesn't want you to miss this special occasion. Your father says please hurry. I am here to watch the sheep."

Jonah warms his hands at the fire.

"Are all my brothers there Jonah?"

"Yes, and they did not appear happy." Jonah frowned at David.

"That does not bode well for me." Joy took that opportunity to scamper into the brush.

"Go David, I will get her." Jonah followed Joy into the fog.

Ashley and Paige came from behind the rocks and Ashley said.

"We need to go to Bethlehem with you. There is nothing for us here on the mountain. The Seal is not here."

David looked at the girls and nodded.

"Follow me. We must be quick. My father never sends for me unless it is important."

Ashley and Paige quickly gathered their things, looked once more at the sheep and then followed David through the fog and down the mountain to Bethlehem.

Chapter 17

Bethlehem. Of all places in the world Ashley thought she would see in her lifetime, Bethlehem would have never made the list. From her Bible history, she knew the city, that was to later be called the City of David, was only about five miles Southwest of Jerusalem. Her heart nearly beat from her chest as she realized that she would unbelievably get to see Samuel, as the Lord's "Kingmaker" anoint David as Saul's successor. How she wished that Paige believed as she did.

Following David down the mountain may also have contributed to her rapidly beating heart. She knew she and Paige would have gotten so lost. David knew the path and even in the dark was able to navigate quickly. She grinned as she listened to Paige's heavy breathing and knew that any moment she would protest.

"Holy cow David! Who the heck pulled your fire alarm? I am not a cross country mountain runner you know. Slow down for Pete's sake." Paige used her tunic sleeve to wipe sweat out of her eyes.

"Man, they don't make sandals like these anymore. I have a pair of Chaco sandals that would not have made it pass the first bend. But oh, how pretty they are." Ashley winks at Paige who gives her the thumbs up sign.

"Holy cows? Chaco? And who is Pete? Where are you girls from? Not Egypt. I think you both dropped down from the sky, and Paige, **you** landed on your head." David laughed at his own joke.

"Hey, watch it sheep boy. You do not want to get me started on the world as you know it."

Paige was practically hyperventilating.

"Really though David, can we stop for a water break? My tongue is practically glued to the roof of my mouth." Ashley bent at the waist, resting her hands on her knees.

"Yes. But not for long. My father and brothers will be waiting." David took out a bag of water and passed it around.

"I have never heard you speak of your brothers other than to answer my question about how close you all were. Are they nice?" asked Ashley'

"Do they look as good as you?" threw in Paige.

"They are all older. Handsome. But they don't really have a lot to do with me. I'm the smelly sheep boy, remember? They all want to be in King Saul's army. Me, I just want to take care of my father's sheep. My brothers think tending sheep is beneath their capabilities. According to them anyone can be a shepherd, but not just anyone can lead an army."

"You are the bravest person I know David. You killed a huge lion with a knife and a sword." Paige's face took on a stern look.

Ashley looked at David and innocently asked.

"Why do you supposed your father sent for you David?"

"I don't know, probably to escort my brothers to Saul's army camp. He probably needs me to see to their things."

"Things?"

"Yes, you know. Food, tents, armor and such."

"They can't take care of their own stuff?"

"Why should they? I always travel with them to help."

Paige was almost indignant.

"Help them! David, they use you like a servant."

"Paige! This is what David is familiar with. Don't create problems we can't fix." Ashley looked a little alarmed.

"Well call it what you will. Wrong is wrong Ashley." Paige had her stubborn look going for her.

"Come on then, we need to get down the mountain. I'm surprised my father hasn't sent someone else for me already." David lifted his knapsack to his shoulder and started down the path.

Following behind David Ashley looked over at Paige and whispered.

"If you are not careful you are going to do or say something that will change history for all time. I want to go home. I don't want to be stuck in a place that never heard of Chaco shoes. I also miss having a bathroom."

"Surely I can't change history to the point of doing away with bathrooms for our future. Don't get all snarly on me. I will watch what I say. But you and I both know that David is being misused. He's going to be a King for crying out loud!"

"Shhhh! Not so loud, he will hear you."

"Gee, does he have to walk so fast? Time is definitely on his side. Boy, is he going to be surprised."

The girls followed David down the mountain and into Bethlehem. Surprises were waiting for all of them.

Chapter 18

Bethlehem was just as Ashley imagined it to be. The sun was high in the sky and the smell of food being cooked over open fires made her mouth water. Her eyes tried to take everything in at a glance and so distracted was she that she almost missed the tall, cute young guy who grabbed David by his shoulder, pulling him through the center of the city. His voice was angry and his hands rough. Cute? Maybe not.

"Paige! Hurry, we will get left behind. We need to follow David."

Paige shot Ashley a glance and said.

"You follow David. I want to look around. The Seal could be anywhere. We will catch up later."

She started toward a stall with colorful, hooded clothes draped around.

"But Paige, it's David's anointing."

Ashley frowned.

"Ashley, you go. Hurry or you will lose David in this crowd. You don't want to miss it."

Paige disappeared into the stall.

"Be careful." But Paige was gone.

Ashley took off toward David's disappearing head. David's brother pushed him inside a large temple. Quiet as a mouse, Ashley tipped toed into the building. She slipped behind a tall pillar that rose to the top of the temple. Several men in Priest like robes stood around.

"These must be the elders of the city." She said to herself.

Two older men stood with six of the cutest guys she had ever seen, all looking at David who was being not so gently shepherded down toward them at the front of the temple.

"Wow! Counting David, we've got eight guys hot and cool looking. Paige is going to hate herself for missing these guys. David is somewhat smaller in stature than his brothers but just as handsome, and going by the attitudes of the brothers, David was kinder, gentler and more approachable. David's brothers were not happy. It seemed clear that they thought Samuel was anointing the wrong brother. It was also clear to me that the Bible spoke truth. "that God sees not as man sees, for man looks at the outward appearance, but the Lord looks at the heart." David was indeed different.

The complete goodness of his heart struck me full on as I watched Samuel, (just as the Bible said) lift the horn of oil and anoint David in the midst of his brothers. Suddenly I remembered all the stories from 1 Samuel. The Bible said the Lord rushed upon David from that day forward.

As my Pastor once said, 'David's brothers were all show and no go. They looked through the eyes of man. God knew what He was doing when He chose David. He sees the heart.'

I wondered then what God sees when He looks at me.

It's an amazing feeling to actually be a witness to such a historical event. Even though I'm far from home, here with a girl I had not even met until this whole finding lost seals thing started. I felt energized and able to conquer any obstacle. My only regret is that Paige did not see.

"Paige! Oh snap! The bull is surely in the china shop. I'd better find her before she erases history, never mind changes it."

Slipping out of the temple was easy since Samuel was talking with David, his family and the elders.

Finding Paige was also easy as all I had to do was follow the angry voices. A stall owner and what appeared to be his wife were shouting and waving their fists angrily at Paige, who was backing out of the stall.

"Paige! What happened?" Ashley grabbed her arm.

"They thought I was going to buy something and when I said I have no money they thought I was trying to steal something. Let's go, I've seen enough!"

Both girls started walking away. They looked back to make sure they weren't being followed by angry store owners or their law keepers.

"We need to find a place to sleep." Paige pointed at a moderately sized building.

"I'll look in here and this side of the street. You take the place there and that side of the street. Yell if you find something."

Ashley nodded and walked into a building.

Paige entered her building easily, there were no doors. Just an open front.

Chapter 19

The building was archaic by any standards. Barnlike but not. Odd tools lined the walls. The center of the building had a pit with a large fire. Smoke spiraled up through a hooded hole in the ceiling to the outside. Stone and wood tables along with wooden benches were close to the fire. An old man was working at the table closest to the fire. With a grunt he held a thin silver object up to the light of the fire. On closer inspection Paige realized the man held a silver chain like necklace.

"That's beautiful." She said to the man.

"You want to buy?" he held the necklace up in the light.

Paige held her hands up in front of her.

"I have no money."

The light of the lantern glinted off her watch. It drew the man's eyes to it.

"You want to trade?"

Paige looked at her watch then at the necklace.

"Sure. I can't remember where or when I got the watch. So yes, I'll trade."

She began to remove the watch from her left wrist.

"Watch?" asked the man, already reaching for it.

"Yes. It tells the time." Paige handed the watch over to the man. She determinedly ignored her twinge of guilt and thoughts of changing history.

The man looked at the watch in amazement. His eyes followed the second hand around the numbers on the watch. The watch itself was large with shiny crystal stones set around the face which was trimmed in a gold color. The band itself was silver and expandable.

Paige felt a little guilty about swapping the cheap watch for the obviously expensive silver necklace, so she asked the man.

"Are you sure you want to trade your silver for my watch?"

Without ever taking his eyes off her watch the man nodded and reached for the wrist watch. He then handed her the silver chain necklace.

Paige looked at the silver chain in her hand and looked up to thank the man but no one was there.

"Hey! Where did you go? I wanted to thank you."

Looking around the work place she knew she was alone. Frowning she said softly.

"Thank you?"

Looking back one more time she shook her head and as she was about to leave she noticed the silver smith's loft. Straw was sticking through the cracks. Her eyes found the ladder. Checking to make sure the straw was in no danger from the fire, Paige made a clicking sound with her mouth and turned to find Ashley. They needed to get to the loft before the silver smith returned to his work. They would be snug and warm in the loft and as long as no one knew they were there, they would be safe.

Chapter 20

Ashley and Paige entered the silver smith's shop as quietly as they could. The silver smith had not yet returned.

"Hurry Ashley. We need to get up in that loft before anyone sees us."

Paige started climbing the ladder with Ashley close behind her.

"Ummm. It's warm and cozy up here." Ashley began to look around.

The loft was stuffy with the smell of smoke and straw, as well as dark. It was reasonably clean. There were noticeable storage items in the back of the loft. The wall on the left had a built- up area that resembled a low bump bed or crib filled with straw. At the end of the area was a stack of rough blankets. The girls hastily covered the straw with blankets, leaving some free to cover up with during the night. The fire would not last all night and they knew by experience how cold it gets in the early hours. It did not escape their attention that the only way up to, and out of the loft was the ladder they came up from initially.

"We need a weapon."

Paige began to look around the loft again, using her hands to feel around.

"A weapon?"

"Yes. We are not completely hidden up here Ashley. What if we are discovered? Not everyone is trust worthy. We have to be able to defend ourselves here."

Chills flew down Ashley's spine.

"That's a scary thought."

Ashley starts looking for a weapon too.

"No. The scary thought would be us defenseless. You have no idea how scary that could be."

"Do you know Paige? Do you personally know how it feels to be defenseless?"

Paige looked confused for a moment.

"I don't know Ashley. I guess I watch a lot of TV. I have no memories of ever having to defend myself. I don't know where that came from."

Paige laughed at herself.

"I just don't want to be caught without a means to defend myself. I don't know these people or what they are capable of."

"Me either. You are, of course, right. Will these do?"

Ashley pulls what resembles modern day pitch forks from a pile of straw in the back corner of the loft. She almost stepped on a prong.

"Perfect. We will put one at the head of our bed and one at the foot. We will sleep head to foot."

"Head to foot?"

Ashley looked puzzled.

"Yeah. Your feet to my head. My feet to your head. You take the fork at your head and I will take the fork at my head. Agreed?"

Ashley nodded. She was already missing the easy nights with David and his sheep.

"If it's not too uncomfortable let's sleep with our shoes on. That way we can run at a moment's notice."

Settling in their straw bed both girls listen to the strange noises of Bethlehem at night.

"Do you think the Seal is in the City?" Paige whispers.

"It is not in the temple. I didn't see it in any of the shops I went into either. It's like trying to find a needle in a haystack."

A noise below alerts the girls to be quiet.

The silver smith was closing up his business for the night. Both girls held their breath, hoping he did not have any reason to look into his loft.

After about thirty minutes of tension filled silence, the girls realized the silver smith had retired for the night and that they were finally alone.

"We need to sleep Ashley. We have to be up early in the morning to be out before the silver smith starts his work."

"Well I guess traveling with David taught us the value of an early start."

"Yeah. I guess he got anointed and all that?"

"It was awesome Paige. History in the making. I'm sorry you missed it."

"I wonder where David is now."

"Probably with his family. I wasn't impressed with his brothers. They were cute but rough with David. I think they didn't like getting passed over by Samuel. I couldn't tell how David's father reacted to Samuel's choice."

"How did David take it?"

"He seemed stunned. He looked around for us you know." There was a smile in her voice.

"Did he? I can honestly say I learned a lot from him. He is incredibly kind, gentle and everlastingly good. I can also say I have never smelt anything as bad as David."

Both girls laughed out loud.

"choose!"

Chapter 21

Ashley couldn't say what it was exactly that woke her up. A whisper of cold. A feeling of evil. She couldn't be sure but she was suddenly wide awake and alert. Paige slept next to her undisturbed.

Listening intently, she heard a noise from the shop floor beneath the loft. Ashley argued with herself about the wisdom of waking Paige. From experience she knew Paige woke loudly and if she was startled she was very loud.

She did not want to alert the intruders below to their presence. She prayed hard that whoever was below would not come up the ladder. It was necessary to stay completely still to prevent straw from dropping between the planking of the loft floor cracks.

"Where is it?" A gruff voice yelled.

"Quiet you imbecile! The shop keeper sleeps in a room at the back. You don't want to wake him. He is very strong."

"Are you sure you saw him working with silver?"

"Yes, yes. Beautiful work."

"Where would he put it? Surely he would not leave such a piece as that lying around for the likes of us to steal it."

The man laughed at his own joke.

"A hiding place maybe. Look everywhere, but be quiet about it."

Ashley heard things moving around.

After what seemed a long time, the voices sounded closer. She tried to be perfectly still and knew that her shaking body could give her presence away.

"There's a loft. Would he have a hiding place up there? we better check because if we find nothing there, then the only place left would be the room he sleeps in. This better not be a wasted run. You swore we would be richer from our efforts."

The threat was there for anyone to hear.

Ashley's stomach tightened into an uncomfortable knot. She knew she had to wake Paige and quickly. She heard the creak of the ladder as someone started up it.

Ashley had just reached for Paige when she heard the silver smith's voice.

"What is going on here?"

There was a lot of scrambling, some oofs and ughs, then silence.

Ashley watched the light of a lantern as it went to the covered door.

"The thieves did not find what they were looking for. They will be back and I will be waiting. The silver chain will be safe from them as long as it stays hidden. That will be up to you. If they find that you have it they will not be kind and may take more than the chain."

Ashley wondered who he could be talking to.

"You girls are safe for tonight. But tomorrow you must find safer sleeping arrangements. And whatever you do, you must keep the chain out of sight."

"He's talking to us." Ashley thought in shock.

"Sleep well girls, God and I are watching over you."

"Thank you, sir."

Then silence filled the silver smith's shop.

"Thank You, Lord, for keeping us safe and for the silver smith's kindness."

Ashley breathed her prayer.

She puzzled over the silver smith's words about the silver chain. Did he think they had stolen it? He did not seem to be upset about it. Did Paige have it? Ashley looked over at Paige and wondered, not for the first time, what did she actually know about her.

"I'm sleeping in a loft on a bed of straw in the City of Bethlehem Mom. But I'm not alone, Paige is here. You would like her Mom, she's funny. She doesn't believe in God though, but I'm hoping that will change. We are in Bethlehem! She has to believe. Who wouldn't believe with King David standing before your eyes. He is personable and kind. The Bible was right on about him. He will make a good King, mistakes and all. Will you keep loving me and looking for me? This is great but I want to come home. I love you. Goodnight Mom. I will figure out how to get home, I promise."

In the words of "Gone With The Wind's" Scarlett O'Hara, 'I'll think about that tomorrow, after all, tomorrow is another day.'

With that epic thought, Ashley snuggled down and went to sleep.

Chapter 22

"Paige! Wake up! We have to go before the Silversmith comes in to start his work. Wake up Paige!"

Paige moans as Ashley pushes her shoulder to wake her.

"Go away, I don't want to wake up. I dreamed of robbers all night last night."

"That was no dream buttercup, we had robbers last night for real."

"Robbers!"

Paige sat straight up.

"We did?"

Paige laughed.

"We did indeed. Seems they were looking for a silver necklace the Silversmith made."

Paige placed her hand at her throat.

"What happened?"

They didn't find the necklace down below and were about to climb up to the loft to look when the Silversmith came in with a sword and the robbers ran."

"Did they know we were up here? You didn't wake me."

"I was afraid you would make a noise and give our presence away. You haven't asked about the necklace."

Paige looked everywhere but at Ashley.

"Paige? Do you know anything about the necklace? Did you take it? Tell me you didn't take it?"

Ashley was looking alarmed.

"I....I."

"Paige!"

"Alright! I have it. But I didn't steal it. Thanks for thinking I did."

"If you didn't steal it, how did you get it?"

"I traded my watch for it. The Silversmith wanted my watch. I wanted the necklace. I tried to tell him it was not a fair trade but he was fascinated with the second hand going around the numbers. I couldn't say no. Please don't make me give it back."

She grabbed the chain at her neck and turned pleading eyes on Ashley. "I don't know."

"It won't change history. The battery will eventually run down and he will forget about the watch. Please Ashley?"

"Fine, but we have to go. The Silversmith knew we were here by the way. Do you know how he knew we were here?"

"No. Did he say anything?"

"He said for us to find safer sleeping arrangements for tonight and to sleep good because he and God were watching over us. He also said for us to keep the necklace out of sight. That's odd, don't you think?"

"Well maybe he thought the robbers would try to take the necklace from us if they broke into his shop to steal it from him."

"The two men who came to rob the place did not sound very friendly or nice. I think they would have killed the Silversmith for the necklace if they had not been surprised by him."

"Did you get a look at them?"

"No, but I heard them. They were real Bonnie and Clyde types."

Ashley shivered.

"Ok, I'm ready to go. I hate that we have to leave this nice warm spot."

"Yeah but if those men come back they will come up here first and I shudder to think what they would do to us if they found us."

Ashley and Paige climbed down the loft ladder and headed for the cloth door.

"What time is it? I don't have my watch."

Paige grinned as she asked the question.

"About 6am our time. They don't know about daylight savings here."

She grinned back at Paige.

"You sure are in a good mood for someone who almost got snatched by two goons. What's up?

"I told my Mom I wasn't alone here because I have you, but I forgot we both have the Lord looking out for us too."

"You talked to your Mom last night?"

"Well not face to face. I air whispered to her."

"Air whispered?"

"I sent my words out in the air to find their way to her ears."

"You are crazy girl. Certifiably coo coo."

"Uh hum."

Both girls laughed as they left the shop.

Chapter 23

The girls ate their breakfast from the bag of manna. Drank water from the City well. Agreeing then to split up and begin their search for the Seal.

"Be on the look out for a place to crash for the night. We should meet up at the well at dusk. I'll put a few pieces of manna in my pocket for lunch. If you have any problems find me and I will do the same."

Ashley looked at Paige for agreement.

"Ok. Be careful."

"Back at ya sister."

"Ashley?" Paige grabbed Ashley's sleeve.

Turning, Ashley looked back at Paige.

"Yeah?"

"Where do you suppose the Seal is hidden?"

"Truthfully, I don't know Paige. Look, why don't we go together. That way when we find it we can leave together. We can start in the temple. Ok?"

"Yeah, sounds good."

People were already coming and going into the temple. It made it easy for the two girls to mix and mingle with them to look around.

"The artwork is beautiful. I noticed that there are no stones in any of it though."

"The men in robes look angry. Do they all look that way or just religious guys?"

Ashley looked in the direction Paige was pointing.

"They look mad and they seem to be looking around for something. We better disappear before they find us. We would have a hard time explaining ourselves to these guys. Here I'm thinking you are guilty and rarely proven innocent."

Both girls quickly slip behind a thick curtain.

"Are you sure the gold was there?"

"Yes, yes. Dropped in the collecting plate not but a short time ago."

"Keep an eye out. I will put a gold coin in the plate and see if we can catch a thief."

Both robed men walked toward the back of the temple.

Ashley and Paige slipped from the curtain into a group of people walking out of the temple.

"Whew!! That was close. I think we will have better luck looking in the shops."

The girls back tracked to the shops and slowly made their way through them looking for God's Seal.

Ashley and Paige were sitting by the City well when they heard their names being called. Looking up both exclaimed with a smile on their face to see David walking towards them.

"David."

"Ashley, Paige. Have you had any luck finding your seal?"

"No, none." They both said at once.

"Well it's getting late. You can both bed down in our stable tonight. My father is sending me with supplies to my brothers in a few days."

"To where the soldiers are fighting?"

"Yes."

"I see. Is it a long way from here?"

"No not long. It's about a half a day's journey. Here is our stable. I will get you blankets. You both should be warm enough here and safe enough."

"Thanks David."

"Yes, thank you David."

David returned with several blankets.

"This should keep you girls warm enough. The straw is much softer than the ground. The only thing missing is Joy inching in between you girls to help keep you warm."

Laughing, the girls wish David a goodnight.

David left them to wrap up in the straw with blankets.

"Paige, we have to go in the morning. You know this is when he kills Goliath. I wouldn't miss that for all the Seals in the world."

Ashley couldn't see Paige roll her eyes in the dark but her tone left nothing to the imagination.

"I want to go home. Finding that stupid Seal is the ticket out of here not watching a mouse catch an elephant with a peanut."

"Well put Paige, well put. But for me can we please leave in the morning early so we can find a good safe place to sleep and if that place also just happens to have an excellent view to Goliath well how lucky would that be? Hum?"

Paige looked at Ashley for a minute or two and finally her face broke into a huge smile.

"Ashley, you are so predictable."

"Predictable?"

"Yeah, like that Insurance commercial. You call and snap! Forget Brad, I just break into my happy dance,"

"I don't get it Paige. Happy dance?"

"It's the little things that make you happy Ashley. We're trying to find a lost Seal, which could be anywhere, so we can maybe go home. You want to watch a small guy kill a huge guy with a pebble and that makes you want to break into your happy dance...... 'Brad, Brad. You love Brad. Nothing can replace Brad. Then the Insurance Company calls and you break into your happy dance'. Get it?"

"Yes. Thanks. I know you could care less but, it's a golden opportunity to see a piece of Biblical history, repeat itself. David killing Goliath was no small thing, excuse the pun. It was a huge thing, again, excuse the pun. I want to see it. Please?"

"Okay, then we get serious about finding the Seal?"

"Absolutely."

"Go to sleep. We have to get up early in the morning. We have a road trip to plan."

"Thanks Paige."

Ashley yawns and curls into her blanket.

"You do know that David will want us to wait until he goes, right?"

"Yeah, but we have to somehow convince him that we will be alright and that we only want to find a safe place to watch from."

"Good luck with that sister. A more protective male than David does not exist."

Chapter 24

"No. it is not safe for the two of you to be alone that close to the camps of all those soldiers."

David was looking stern as he shook his head from side to side.

"We will stay out of sight. The Seal was not on your mountain and it wasn't in Bethlehem. It has to be somewhere. God sent us here for a reason. We have a responsibility to find the missing Seal and we can't do it here. I'm sorry David but we have to go."

David took on a stubborn look.

"Fine but you go when I go."

Paige decided to get in on the action.

"We can't stay with you David. You will be in the camp with your brothers and we will stick out like sore thumbs."

"Sore thumbs? You didn't tell me your thumbs were sore."

"No. Our thumbs aren't sore. What I meant was we would look out of place in your camp. Even with our heads covered it would not take the soldiers long to realize we were girls. No, we can't stay with you. It would be safer for us to hide close by and hope we get a clue as to where to look for the Seal."

David, continuing to be stubborn said.

"From just being around you two for a short time has shown me that you can't stay away from trouble. It finds you. And what about the evil one? He is looking for you two as well."

Ashley frowned for a minute and then looked determined.

"We have a God given task to accomplish and we can't worry about the shadow of evil. We have to go David, please don't try to stop us."

David was silent for a moment and then said'

"I can't get in your way. God's path for you is clear. I will have someone take you and help find a safe place to camp. I will be coming when my father decides to send me. I will find you then. Be safe and stay out of trouble."

"Thank you, David." Both girls said at once.

"Take the blankets I gave you last night. It gets cold on the mountain. No fires. Someone will see and come check. That's from either camp and we don't want that."

"NO!" the girls said together.

David nodded and then walked away.

"That was close." Paige laughed and started folding her blankets.

The girls gathered their things together, making sure they had their bag of manna tucked safely in the big pocket of Paige's cloak.

"When do you suppose we will be leaving? Wonder how far it is, they don't have cars here."

Paige slumped back against the wall unlady like.

"I don't know when we will leave but David said it was half a day's journey and my leg muscles are getting the workout of their young lives. Maybe I will go out for track when we get home."

Ashley grinned at Paige.

"I think I want to be a sheep farmer." Paige said, tongue in cheek.

Paige grinned at Ashley.

"Yeah, we could be partners."

Both girls laughed out loud at their crazy suggestions and then Paige said.

"Seriously. I am thinking I might want to study to be a Veterinarian."

"That idea crossed my mind too Paige. Do you suppose we could maybe study together?"

"That would be great. We just need to find those Seals and get home."

"Right. Somebody is coming."

David and a younger boy walked into the stable.

"This is Abram. He is going to take you both to a place on the mountain that is located between the two camps. You will be high enough to see into the valley below and protected by large boulders. You cannot have a fire at night because both camps will be able to see it if you did. I'll send enough blankets to keep you warm. You will be ok in daylight because of the sun. oh, and I'm sending several water flasks. I will find you later. My father will be sending me any day now. Please be careful and stay out of sight and out of trouble."

"We will do our best David."

"Yeah David, thank you for this. We appreciate all the help you have given us. I don't know where we will find the Seal but when we do find it, it will be because of all you have done for us. We, neither of us, will forget you David."

Paige snickered.

"How can we forget. You're in the….. ummph! Ouch Ashley! That hurt!"

"Sorry. We have to go. We will see you later David. Thanks again for your help."

David looked confused for a moment and then turned to Abram.

"Take care of them Abram and thank you."

David and Abram did the one arm manly hug with the back slap and we started on our journey.

Chapter 25

"I don't think my feet have ever been this dirty before, even when I was a kid. How much longer before we get there? I'm tired, hungry and I've gotta go to the bathroom. Gosh!! My feet hurt too. I think I have a blister on my heel the size of Texas."

Paige looked like a wilted flower and was literally dragging.

"I'm sorry Paige. How can you tell the blister is the size of Texas? You have so much dirt on your feet."

Ashley laughed.

"Ashley! Don't make fun of me. I need to rest. Is that a dust storm ahead?"

All three of them looked down the dirt road at the large cloud of dust.

Abram stopped and looked at the girls.

"That's soldiers from the Israeli camp going home for a rest. We have to hide."

Looking around for a place to go Abram motions for the girls to follow him.

Quickly ducking behind several clumps of bushes off the dirt road the girls and Abram drop down just as the soldiers draw even with them. Most of them teenagers and some not much older than their early twenties. The soldiers are laughing and talking about what they plan to do when they get home, eat till they drop, see their girl, sleep a week and on and on.

Ashley's thoughts are that no matter the time, the place or the war, soldiers the world over were the same. Tears fill her eyes as she thinks of home and the soldiers there that stand between her and the Goliaths of the world. Thank you for your service will not be sufficient for her to say anymore. It will forever more be "Thank you for your sacrifice".

The last of the soldiers walked past their hiding place. Abram held them there for a little longer to be sure that all the soldiers had passed by before he motioned for the girls to come out and that it was safe to continue their journey.

Ashley looked at Paige and burst out laughing. Paige returned the look and laughed too.

"If you are laughing at what I think you are laughing at you should see yourself. If I have as much dust on my face as you do on yours then we are indeed dirty."

Abram ran a finger down his cheek and laughed at the amount of dirt on it. The girls laughed harder because he left a finger size streak down his cheek.

"You girls are a lot of trouble. Let's get going. David will have my hide if I let anything happen to you."

Laughing the girls follow Abram as he once again takes the lead and continues down the dusty, dirt road.

"I'm still tired, hungry and very dirty."

Paige did not sound as whiney as before so Ashley kept quiet and continued to walk behind Abram.

"What time do you think it is now Ashley?"

"I don't know. The sun is not straight over us so I know it is not noon yet."

"Noon? What strange talk is this? Our journey's end is not far off. David sent food so we can find a safe and shady place to eat and rest for a while and then continue our way. I have extra water to wash with. This I know will make you feel better. I have sisters. They hate dirt. David and I would have made the journey without stopping. I get all the hard work. If I thought I had to take my sisters on such a journey as this I would join the soldiers and risk death."

Ashley and Paige were so shocked they stopped walking. Then both of them nearly collapsed laughing. It was Abram's turn to look shocked. Then he too laughed.

"I understand. I sounded like Paige did I not?"

Paige stopped laughing and stared at both Abram and Ashley. This made them laugh more.

"This is a good place to rest and eat."

Abram walked through some trees and down a little hollow to a grassy place. It looked like he had been there before because Abram walked to a fallen tree and sat down with his back to the tree.

Ashley and Paige dropped down beside Abram and accepted the cloth wrapped food he extended to them.

"What is this?" Paige asked.

"Cheese and mutton."

"Don't say a word Paige. Just eat."

"The manna…"

"Eat what has been provided by David. You never know. You might like it and the manna will still be here if you don't."

"Well the cheese is the same as what we ate on the mountain."

Paige bit into the portion of meat and chewed.

"It's different. Not awful. Definitely not my favorite. Chewy. How is yours Ashley?"

Speaking with a mouthful Ashley covers her mouth with her hand and says.

"The same. A coke would be good right now."

"Coke?" Abram looked up with a puzzled face.

"A kind of drink from home."

"And home is where?"

"Paige?"

"Our home is far from here. I am going to rest my eyes for a minute. Without sun glasses the sun is hard on the eyes."

"Sun glasses?"

"Yikes! Can't a girl talk without being questioned about every little thing she says?"

Abram looks at her for a minute and then turns to Ashley.

"I do not know how David understands you girls. You both speak strangely and you do not act as we act. You are nice and do not seem to be dangerous but you are different."

"The world we come from is great because of the difference of her people. Think how boring it would be if we were all alike. Difference is refreshing. With difference comes ideas and that makes changes. Changes makes life very interesting and challenging. New things come from the most unlikely source sometimes. I will forever have a respect for all things different."

"Well said Ashley. You should be in politics."

"Thank you, Paige. Politics is not for me."

"Well, this has been different? We need to finish our journey so I can get you girls to a safe place. I have the return journey also."

"Will you spend the night on the mountain and start home in the morning?"

"No. No, my journey home will be faster alone. I will get home in time for the night meal. Are we ready to go?"

Feeling the relief in his voice at not having to travel with the girls, home, both Ashley and Paige follow Abram once more with a grin on their faces.

"Thank you, Abram, for the meal and the rest."

Abram nods at Ashley and continues to walk.

It is not long before Abram changes direction and it becomes an up-hill walk.

"You know Ashley. Michael did us a favor by depositing us on the mountain instead of making us walk up it. This is a killer hike. I'm wondering where my next breath is coming from."

"I'm regretting that I didn't make better uses of PE in school. Wonder what they use here for charley horses?"

"Charley horses? You girls are really strange."

"Ashley do you suppose they will remember any of this when we are gone?"

"Paige, I'm just hoping I will remember this when we are gone."

"Me too Ashley, me too."

After what felt like an hour's climb up Mount Everest Abram began to slow down. Looking from side to side he walks over to two boulders in a flat area.

"There is a space between these rocks that you girls can put your blankets to sleep. I will check and make sure there are no snakes or spiders."

"Please make sure of that Abram." Both girls shuddered.

"It's safe. Remember to speak softly as sound carries and no fires. The rocks will keep the wind off of you at night and provide protection also from night animals. The valley you see below is the battle ground. The

Philistine camp is in that direction." Abram pointed to the left. "And the Israeli camp is in that direction." He pointed right. "It may be possible to be seen if you stand close to the edge so don't."

"Of course, Abram. We will do as you say. We both thank you for bringing us here. Please be safe on your return journey home." Ashley smiles at the boy. Paige turns to him.

"I hope we didn't cause you too much trouble Abram."

"No, you didn't. Although I can't say I will miss your plaintive voice asking for water, rest, feet rub, a horse and the many other requests. Goodbye. Be safe. David will journey this way soon."

Chapter 26

After Abram was gone the girls began to get their sleeping area arranged to satisfy them both.

"Did Abram say where the bathroom was located?" Paige's tongue in check question made them both laugh.

"We need to look around. I would like to know where the soldier's camps are in relation to where we are. The valley is in front of us, perfect for seeing history in the making. I will check out the camp on the right, you go left. Paige, please be careful and as quiet as you can. We of all things do not want to get caught by either camp."

"No kidding Sherlock. You be careful too. See you back here in a bit. Deal?"

"Deal."

Ashley quietly made her way through the trees and bushes to the mountain's edge. She could smell the smoke from the Israeli camp as well as the food cooking over the open fires. Guards were stationed at the base of the mountain and all over the camp. Tents were everywhere. Soldiers were laughing and talking, joking with each other. Everyone seemed to be at their ease. To look at them you would not think they were being threatened by a large giant called Goliath. Ashley decided she had seen enough. She began to ease back toward her camp when she stepped on a broken limb that snapped like a gunshot. She heard a shout from below and quickly looked around for a hiding place. Closer to the edge than she really wanted to go was a tree with it's roots exposed. The exposed roots hide a hole in the earth large enough for her to crawl into. Sinking down below the tree she prayed she would not be discovered. She nearly screamed when a large arm reached above her head using the limb to help leverage himself up from the side of the mountain. The soldier never once looked down into the hole for he would surely have seen her if he had. She held her breath and closed her eyes. The shadow of evil never scared her as much as this did. There was a shout from below and the soldier near her answered.

"No one here. It was probably a limb from a tree falling to the ground. Yes, here is the limb. I told you it was nothing. I'm coming back down. I'm hungry enough to eat a bear. You girls catch me if I fall now."

There was laughter and sounds of the soldier climbing back down the side of the mountain.

"I told you boys, those Philistines are not smart enough to spy on us. They think their Champion has us running scared. We will show them, yes sir. Saul will see to it. Remember I said it first."

There was more laughter and then silence.

Ashley waited a while and then began to crawl out from her hiding place to quickly and quietly return to her own camp.

Paige, who was on the other side of the mountain saw the Philistine camp but compared to the Israeli camp it was quiet as a church. The soldiers walked around but there was no laughing or joking going on. Their faces looked serious and mean. The camp looked like it was bedding down for the night which reminded her that she and Ashley needed to do the same. She turned and quietly walked back to her and Ashley's camp to find out what Ashley had seen.

Each girl took care of their necessities as David called them and settled on their blankets between the large boulders.

"You first Ashley." Paige maneuvered herself into a comfortable position and waited for Ashley to do the same.

"The Israeli camp was bursting with soldiers. They were loud, laughing and joking. You would have thought they were having a college boy's party. Camp fires everywhere. Look to your right. The sky is practically lit up. Oh, and I was almost caught."

"Ashley!"

"It's alright. I hid. I stepped on a dry, broken limb and it sounded like a gunshot. I scared myself. I hid in a hole covered with tree roots. The soldier who climbed up to investigate practically bragged that the Philistines would not try to spy on them. He said Saul would take care of the problem. I would really like to see their faces when David kills Goliath. I bet that would be something to see."

"Ashley, please be more careful in future. You are the brains of our team and I would not make it out of here without you."

Paige's eyes were bright with unshed tears.

"Don't worry Paige. God will take care of us. And before you deny the existence of God, tell me what you saw."

"Well, yes, the Philistine camp was very quiet. No laughter or joking anywhere. They looked serious as they got the camp ready for the night. I'd say they were pretty scary. Men not boys.

I would not want to bump into one of them day or night."

"Did you see Goliath?"

"No."

Darkness descended as if someone drew the curtain down. The sky lit up with stars.

Ashley looked up at the stars putting on a spectacular display in the heavens.

"It's so beautiful it makes my heart hurt."

Paige looked at the sky and then at Ashley and replied.

"I know. Do you suppose our families are looking at these same stars and wondering where we are?"

"My Papaw once told me that God put the stars in the sky so I would always know that I am never alone. That if I ever got lost I could look up at them and know that he was also looking at them and would find me. I don't think he will be able to find me here."

"He sounds nice."

"Oh, Paige he is. But I gotta tell ya... he has his moments. He and my Nana fit together like cheese and crackers. My Nana is very independent and my Papaw is very protective. Nana will decide she is going somewhere and then announce she is going alone and Papaw says...'oh no you aren't'... she knows he won't let her go by herself but she likes to push his buttons. He knows this and lets her. Cheese and crackers. I miss them too."

"Wonder why I can't remember my family."

"Maybe you hit your head.... wait a minute. I forgot who I was talking to. You are very hard headed."

"Ha Ha. but seriously, what's going on with me? I am real aren't i?"

"Yes Pinocchio. You are a real girl."

Ashley's face was full of laughter.

"I'm serious Ashley. I really can't remember anything before I got here with you."

"I know Paige. I don't understand why you can't remember either, but it's ok. We will figure it out."

"I know. I'm ok."

"We might as well get comfortable."

Ashley began to settle down on the soft ground between the two large boulders she and Paige were hiding in.

"Thank the Lord for David's blankets." That was said as she pulled a blanket tighter around both of them.

"David's blanket my foot! This is Joy's blanket." Paige laughed softly.

"This blanket smells just like that crazy wonderful lamb." Paige wiped at the dampness on her cheeks.

"Oh Paige you…"

"No."

The one word wiped the joy from Ashley's face.

"But Paige, after all we've seen and heard you have to believe a little bit." Pleading eyes looked into doubting eyes.

"Ashley, get real, will you? This has got to be a dream. Of course, it looks like the real thing, but you have to face the facts. Even without all my memories I know that we both must have been taught stories from the Bible. We are either dreaming or we have stepped into a time warp or a tear in time or something. Frankly, I prefer to think we are dreaming since I do not believe the Bible is truth. Even if the Bible is truth how did we get here? The Bible is history… done… over… yet here we are. I know for sure I don't believe in time travel so, 2+2=4… it's a dream."

Seeing the sadness in Ashley's eyes, Paige grabs her hands.

"But hey… it doesn't really matter. We are here… where ever here is, no matter how we got here and we're together, we're safe, at the moment, and we're warm and we have plenty of these fluffy things to eat. We don't have coke but we do have water. Smile… please? For me?"

Ashley smiled through wet tears and said.

"Paige, if we get home… no, when we get home, let's stay friends. I feel I've known you always."

Paige pushed Ashley's shoulder.

"Ahhh, popular, you probably saw me at school and looked through me without really seeing me."

"Paige, I really hope that's not true, but I see you now and I don't want to lose you. You are my very best friend. Please?"

"You're serious. You want me for a BFF? I wish I could remember if I ever had a best friend."

"Paige! Be serious yourself." Ashley laughed.

"Ashley? I know this is changing the subject but, what is so important about these Seals anyway?"

Ashley looked thoughtful for a minute and then said.

"Well, I'll try to explain as best as I can. You see, in heaven, there is a book…"

"The book in the treasure chest!"

"Yes. The book is sealed with seven Seals. Of course, it is really a scroll sealed with seven Seals. You know, like wax seven Seals."

"But we saw a book, not a scroll. The Seals were gone. If it was really a scroll with seven Seals, wouldn't whoever has taken the Seals, taken the scroll or book too?"

"Well, you would think so. We are looking for seven actual silver Seals. I'm thinking for us some things are symbolic."

"Symbolic for what?"

"I'm working on that. Let me tell you why they are so important. In the end times…."

Paige rolled her eyes and started to speak. Ashley held up her hand and said.

"Wait. Just let me finish. In the end times there will be seven years of tribulation. Seven really bad years for the people on earth. False gods, war, famine, unspeakable death, earthquakes and finally Jesus will return. Then the final battle of Armageddon."

Paige interrupts Ashley with a question.

"But when does Jesus start breaking the Seals?"

"At the beginning of the seven years."

"Does He break them all at the same time?"

"No. John MacArthur says Seals one through four are opened in the first three and a half years. The fifth Seal stretching from the first half into the second half and six through seven in the last three and a half."

"Who is John MacArthur?"

"He is a very well- known Pastor and author from California."

"Oh, ok. Can just anybody open the Seals?"

"No. Only Jesus is worthy to open the Seals. He paid for the right with His blood."

"Wait a minute! The first Seal is what?"

"The Conqueror. The white horse with a rider carrying a sword and wearing a crown. False gods, kinda like Goliath."

"Yeah. David is also like a conqueror. He did kill the lion. Kinda symbolic huh?"

"Yep!" Ashley laughed.

Paige looked puzzled for a minute and then said.

"Why are we looking for seven symbolic Seals Ashley?"

"Isn't it obvious? We must have something to learn."

"Well, if that's true, they can just send me home now. I for one, am not buying what they are selling. Just shoot me now and get it over with. I don't need to see David kill Goliath. You know if we were home right now and David killed Goliath, he would probably never be King and spend his days in prison."

"I know, right? But seriously, don't be so melodramatic. Don't you get it? I wrote my paper on the battle of Armageddon. It must be me that has something to learn. You are just along for the ride for some reason. To help me maybe? I just need to figure out what I have to learn so we can go home. We need to come up with a plan to find that Seal without getting ourselves killed in the process."

"Amen sister! I'm all for not getting killed."

Ashley looked over at Paige and touched her hand.

"You are the very best of best friends Paige. I can say for sure that I have learned, that going through life without that special friend is not worth it. My Nana's best friend is Teresa. Friends for over thirty years. They have stuck by each other through school, marriage, babies, distance, cancer and recovery. They would do anything for each other. They are like two teenage girls when they get together. You should hear them laughing. Teresa is much loved by us all and is a very dear friend to Nana. My Nana said if I ever found a friend like that, I was to hold on to her forever. God only sends one special friend not related by blood and it would be up to me to recognize her and hold on. Now I can say I have found that best friend."

"Best friends? Wow! It's a deal Sheep Girl. Best friends forever, however long that is."

"Sheep girl? Have you even smelled yourself lately? Pugh!" Ashley held her nose.

"Ahh... that's lamb e ode cologne. It's all the rage in Bethlehem. I'll bet we'll miss Joy lamb around 3am when we're freezing to death." Paige pretends to shiver.

"That lamb was better than an electric blanket."

Both girls settled the blanket closer around them, settling in for a long cold night. Each girl dreaming of home and wondering if they'll ever see their families again.

Chapter 27

Sunrise.

Ashley and Paige looked up to the Eastern sky as the beginning rays of the sun peeked it's head up over the tops of the tall trees far beyond the large boulders they were hiding between. The beauty of the sunrise caught at Ashley's throat and brought instant tears to her eyes as memories of home flew at a rapid pace through her mind's eye.

"Mama." Slipped out of her lips almost like a prayer.

"Yes." Replied Paige with tears of her own dropping off her nose.

Hands met midway and both girls acknowledged the beginnings of a true friendship. Familiar noises began to stir the air all around them. Sheep talking to one another, birds stirring from their nests looking for food, a large giant like man stomping across the field...

"Wow! Would you look at that? Now there is something you don't see every day."

Paige almost stood up in her excitement.

"Goliath. He is a big man. Don't stand up... he'll see you!" Ashley grabbed Paige's cloak and pulled her back behind the boulder.

"In a million years I would never have believed I would have a front row seat watching David slaying Goliath with the old sling shot event. Who would have known."

Shaking her head Paige looked at Ashley with all kinds of excitement shining in her eyes.

Ashley wisely reframed from reminding Paige that she didn't believe the event ever took place in the first place. But she was right when she said...'who would have known'?"

"We have to be focused Paige. The Seal has to be here somewhere. I can't imagine where but it wasn't anywhere we went with the sheep and it wasn't anywhere to be found at David's anointment. It wasn't in Bethlehem. It has to be here somewhere. Be sharp, look alive, be alert and don't let anyone see you or it's curtains for us."

"Let's get closer. I want a better view. See that group of rocks over there close to the edge? Let's see if we can get between the two largest ones for a closer look. Up close Goliath will probably be something to see. Wish I had my cell phone. Pictures speak louder than words. Nobody is gonna believe this. Heck, I don't even believe it and I'm seeing it. Come on Ashley, crawl."

Chapter 28

"What are we doing here again? I can't believe it was my idea to get closer."

This was said with a grunt from Paige as the two girls were crawling through grass and shrub bushes toward two large rocks wedged together at the edge of the mountainside. There was a large crack between the rocks allowing a perfect view of the valley below. Two separate sets of smoke rose into the sky from each end of the valley marking the sites of the two camps, the Israelites and the Philistines.

As Ashley crawled, she knew she would have bruises and scratches on her arms and legs from the hard grass and bushes they were passing through but she didn't care. Just as she didn't care that her excitement was clearly causing her breathing to be erratic as she replied to Paige.

"We have a front row seat to witness one of the most extraordinary historical events to ever happen. An event that most people don't even believe happened at all."

"Tell me about it, girlfriend." Paige grunted as she crawled over a rock with her knee.

"Sorry, I forgot who I was talking to. But seriously Paige, you can't deny what's right in front of you."

"Butt."

"But what?" Ashley interrupted.

"Your butt, that's what is right in front of me... ugh... what is that smell?" Paige began to stand up.

"Get down Paige! The Philistines will see you. Crawl into this crevice, we can see better."

Ashley crawled between the rocks and looked down into the valley.

"The Philistines are cooking some kind of animal on a spit."

"Ashley, it still has its insides… ugh, nasty. That's what smells so bad. That's disgusting and they're gross."

Suddenly the ground began to shake. The girls hugged each other thinking the mountainside was about to fall into the valley below and them along with it when they were cast into darkness.

"What the…"

"Sshh, Paige, look!" Both girls looked between the crack in the rocks. A giant stood with his back to the mountain. He was so tall he blocked out the sun making it dark between the rocks.

"Oh my!"

"Goliath."

"He's bigger than the Pillsbury Doughboy on Ghostbusters." Paige snickered.

"If he huffed and puffed he could blow down our rocks."

"Get serious Paige. He is one mean killing machine."

The ground started shaking again as the giant started walking across the valley.

Ashley watched as if mesmerized. Paige watched the giant move with a silly grin on her face.

In a quiet voice Ashley quoted from the Bible.

"Then a champion came out from the armies of the Philistines named Goliath, from Gath…"

"Look at the size of him! Look Ashley! What in the name of peace is he wearing?"

Ashley continued to quote.

"whose height was 6 cubits and a span…"

"In English Ashley!" Paige said in disgust.

"Some think he's over eleven and three and a half feet tall. He's wearing a bronze helmet and a scale armor that weighs about one hundred and twenty five pounds. He has bronze greaves on his legs and a bronze javelin slung between his shoulders. The shaft of his spear is like a weavers' beam and the head of his spear weighs about fifteen pounds. See that person in front of him? He's his shield carrier."

Ashley's eyes never left Goliath.

"Eleven feet tall huh?"

"Paige?" Ashley spoke but Paige ignored her and continued to talk.

"Wow, he is one ugly man. Did you see his eyes? Now I understand the meaning of cold dead eyes. It's like he doesn't have any feelings. He sure is sure of himself, listen."

"Paige?" Paige continued to ignore Ashley. Looking everywhere in her excitement.

Goliath stood before his armies shouting at the armies of Israel.

"Why do you come out to draw up in battle array? Am I not the Philistine and you servants of Saul? Choose a man for yourselves and let him come down to me." Goliath stretched out his arms as he was shouting and when he hit his chest with his hand it sounded like thunder.

Both girls jumped as if struck by lightning.

Goliath continued his threats.

"If he is able to fight with me and kill me, then we will become your servants; but if I prevail against him and kill him, then you shall become our servants and serve us."

Goliath raised his big meaty fist and shook it at the Israelites. He turned and stomped back towards his camp. The shield carrier walked backwards after Goliath.

"What a show!"

"Paige?"

"No one is gonna believe this. Oh my gosh! I don't even believe it. What next?"

Ashley took one last look at Goliath and turned to Paige.

"We need to find David."

"David? Why?"

Paige had a puzzled look on her face.

"Because time is running out. There are still things we need to learn from David, and I found the Seal."

Ashley started crawling back towards the way they had come.

"What do you mean? I thought we were here to find the Seal. What more could we possibly learn from a time forgotten shepherd boy? YOU FOUND THE SEAL? WHERE?"

"You forget, that time forgotten shepherd boy became King David of Judah. Jesus, the true King came from his linage. Honestly Paige, how can you not know that?"

Ashley shook her head and kept crawling.

Paige's knee hit another rock and she picked it up and threw it with fury. Her voice was sharp as she fired back at Ashley.

"When are you going to learn that this world is made up with all kinds of people. You believe and I don't. you believe this is all real and I don't. There are short people and tall people, Black, White, Asian, Hispanic, and don't forget Country Folks, oh yeah and Cajuns. Get a grip Ashley, David can't teach me a thing. Maybe I can teach him a thing or two though."

Paige kept moving behind Ashley.

"What do you mean? What are you talking about?"

Ashley swung her head around to look at Paige.

"Well, I technically know what happens next don't I? don't you think David would like to know?"

Paige looked and sounded slightly smug.

Ashley stopped where she was and Paige ran into her.

"Hey!"

"Don't Paige. I don't know but you could change history. Please don't say anything to David. I want to go home."

"Then let's get the Seal and get out of here. Where is it?"

Ashley looked at Paige for a moment.

"You won't say anything?" tears ran down her cheeks.

Paige looked down at the ground. She hated to see Ashley cry.

"No, but let up on the preaching, "Yes." will you?"

Satisfied, Ashley turned and started crawling again.

"I'm sorry Paige."

"I'm sorry too Ashley."

Crawling behind Ashley Paige said.

"These rocks and stickers are killing me." She looks down at her hands.

"I need a manicure. Where is the Seal?"

"A bathtub sounds like heaven to me. It's amazing what we take for granted. As soon as I get home I'm going to drink a large pepsi and eat a hamburger while I'm soaking in my tub."

"Pizza, yeah Pizza sounds good to me. The Seal?"

"Oh, yeah. It's in Goliath's shield. In the center of it."

"How did you notice that?"

"The sun caught it and it winked at me."

"Okay, great. Let's go get it so we can go home. How are we going to get it did you say?"

"I don't know. I have to think. We can't do anything until tomorrow. It's afternoon now, the sun was straight overhead about an hour or so ago. I'm hungry. Let's eat and think this thing through. Does that sound like a plan?"

"As good as any."

The girls crawled between the boulders onto their blankets, ate and drank their water. Each of them very much lost in their thoughts. Ashley was thinking about how Paige lost her temper. Paige was thinking about that too but with shame. For a moment David and Goliath was forgotten as each girl wondered how they were going to get their closeness back.

"I'm sorry." Both girls said at the same time.

"You first Paige."

"I'm truly sorry. I would never say or intentionally do anything that would cause a change in history. I so very much want all of this to end and for both of us to be at home where we belong.

I don't want there to be a coolness between us or a disagreement. We have to work together not against each other. I'm so sorry. Will you please forgive me?"

"I forgive you if you'll forgive me. I'm sorry too. I know I can be overbearing sometimes and pushy about certain things. I'll back off. I can't make you believe in something that I believe in and honestly, it's not even my job anyway. You are right, we need to work together. Let's rest and think about how to get the Seal. We can share ideas in the morning. Is that okay?"

"Sounds like a plan. I'm going to the little girl's bush. I'll be back in a bit."

Paige had a plan but needed some information before she acted on it. She took care of her personal business and then quietly made her way to the Philistine's side of the mountain.

She walked the entire length of the side facing the camp. She was looking for the easiest and safest way down into the camp. She would need to enter the camp early before sunrise while everyone was asleep, sneak into the shield barrier's tent and get the Seal out of the shield. shield. Easy, peasey. Oh yeah. she'll need to do all that and not get caught. First order of business is to find out which tent belongs to the shield carrier.

Movement in front of a small tent caught her eye. Quickly Paige ducked behind a bush and laying on her stomach peered down over the side of the mountain. The shield carrier! He was carrying Goliath's armor into his tent. How convenient that his tent is so close to the mountain.

Armed with all the information she thought she needed, Paige made note of where she needed to crawl down the mountain.

She found her way back to their boulder camp and made herself comfortable to wait for dawn. She had a Seal to retrieve. Ashley will be so surprised.

Chapter 29

Paige crawled through the tall grass to look over the side of the mountain into the camp of the Philistines. Most of their fires had burned low as the sun had not come up yet. The camp was quiet, everyone asleep with no one stirring around as yet. The posted guards that she could see were sleeping on their feet with their backs against trees or rocks. The only guards she could see that were awake stood either side of a large tent opening. It had to be Goliath's tent. Inching closer to the edge to get a better look, Paige felt the ground she was laying on begin to crumble underneath her. Quickly turning over and around Paige began to sink a little and then suddenly she began to slide down into a crevice, feet first. She was hidden from view by the bushes and trees growing into the side of the mountain. She was covered to the waist in dirt and debris and could feel roots at her feet.

She knew at once it was going to be difficult getting out of the waist deep dirt and impossible to get out if her feet got tangled in the roots. Her worst fear was being seen by the Philistines and capture.

Her brain was in overdrive trying to decide what to do first, when she was hit with a bone deep cold wave that passed through her and left her feeling lost and hopeless.

Two things occurred to her at once. "So that's what Ashley has been talking about. The shadow of evil and oh snap! I'm in deep trouble."

But thinking she was in trouble was nothing compared to the reality of actually being in trouble, for in a branch high over her head was a very large snake and he was hissing at her. The snake was hissing and moving in her direction.

A fear such as Paige has never known crawled up her spine.

Trying to keep her feet from dropping down into the roots, Paige began to move dirt and debris from around her waist.

Keeping an eye on the snake, which was getting closer and an eye on the Philistine camp, Paige knew she was running out of time. When the sun comes up the camp will wake and without a doubt she will be discovered. That is if the snake doesn't kill her first.

"Well snap! This is another fine mess you've gotten yourself into. How in the name of all that is possible are you going to get yourself out of this mess.

Where is Wonder Woman when you need her." Paige starts to sing softly.

"All our hopes are pinned upon you and the magic that you do. Stop a bullet cold, make the axis fold, change their minds and change the world… you're a wonder, Wonder Woman."

Then reality sets in and finally with tears Paige says.

"Oh fudge, I am truly stuck here and it's my own fault. I just had to be the super hero of the day and retrieve the Seal and look where that got me. That snake is not stopping and is definitely getting closer. He looks mean, hungry and mad. This is not going to end well for me. Okay, I admit it. I don't know what to do. The only person I have in the world right now is sound asleep and doesn't know that I'm not asleep too.

Michael? Can you hear me? Will you help me out of here? Between me and you, I'm really scared of snakes and I really don't want to die here in this world. Can you wake Ashley up and tell her to bring a rope or something? Please? I want out of here!"

A sound from below her causes her to freeze. Then laughter causes her to be very silent. Two soldiers walking the perimeter of the camp come into view. Paige can barely see them through the bushes. Hoping that if she can't see them clearly that they can't see her at all.

The snake takes this opportunity to make his presence known to the soldiers and shakes the rattlers on his tail.

Tears well up in Paige's eyes as all the color leaves her face.

"Would you look at the size of that snake!"

"Yeah, what a kill. I think I can just reach that thing with my sword."

"Don't bother, we need to get moving."

"Oh no, I could not shut my eyes wondering where that thing was crawling too and in whose bed he might land in. would you want him in your bed?"

"You're right… kill him."

"I'm just going to climb up a bit using this tree limb to hold me steady."

The soldier started climbing up towards the snake, never seeing Paige, who had become as still as a stature. When the soldier reached and grabbed the tree limb his arm was under Paige's nose. The overwhelming smell caused Paige to gag. She immediately held her breath for fear he could feel it on his arm.

With one swift swipe of his sword, the soldier cut the snake's head off. Paige nearly fainted as the head and body of the snake fell on her.

"Now, just to get the thing to show around camp."

Paige then knew real fear. The tears in her eyes fall to her cheeks.

"No, the Champion is rising. We better finish our rounds. Come back for the snake later. It's not like it's going anywhere." He laughed.

The tears on Paige's cheeks began the short journey to their fall. Paige went into full panic mode. Her thoughts were filled with terror.

"Don't fall, don't fall, don't fall."

"Right, what is that awful smell? It's like sheep dung. This place stinks."

"Yeah, yeah. Let's get going."

The soldier moves his arm just as the first tear drops to the ground. The two soldiers continue on their round of the camp perimeter.

Paige is finally able to take a good deep breath, tears left dirty tracks down her otherwise white face.

"Paige!"

Paige looks up to see Ashley looking down from the top of the mountain.

"Paige! Where are you?"

"Here Ashley! I'm down here. Please be careful, the mountainside is trying to collapse."

"Where Paige? I can't see you."

"I'm in dirt up to my waist and covered by bushes. Thank goodness."

"I'm coming down."

"Please be careful, the next time the earth moves it won't be just my feet feeling it. It will probably bury me."

Ashley drops down next to Paige.

"Watch the snake."

"Snake!!"

Ashley was half way back up the mountain before she heard Paige say.

"It's dead Ashley. The soldier killed it."

"Soldier! Oh my, Paige. What have you done?"

"Nothing! Just get me out of here."

"Okay, okay, keep your britches on. I'm coming. But you've got a lot of splaining to do Lucy."

All Ashley heard in reply was a hiccough. Once Ashley was beside Paige again and pushing dirt around Paige said.

"How did you find me?"

"I don't know. One second, I was sound asleep and the next I was wide awake. I suddenly felt like you were in trouble. This just seemed like the place to look for you."

"Well, it was either Michael or Wonder Woman."

"If those are my choices, I'll take Michael for two thousand Alex."

"Ha, Ha."

"Right, almost got you dirt free."

"Thanks."

"You know I mean figuratively speaking right? But you're welcome. You can't keep the snake."

Paige shivered.

"That was very scary, not to mention the soldiers."

"Soldiers? There were more than one? Come on. Can you get out now?"

Paige was out of the hole and climbing like a monkey up the side of the mountain.

"Be careful. We don't want to loosen any more dirt. We'll both be buried then. I'm right behind you. You do want to hurry though. The Philistine camp is coming alive and it looks like a soldier headed this way."

The girls reached the top just as they heard.

"Looks like the mountainside is trying to come down. I'm getting the snake before it is covered up. You are one big slithering thing."

The soldier shuddered,

"I would not want you for abed mate that's for certain. Let's go have some fun."

Chapter 30

Sitting on her blanket between the large boulders Paige begins to inspect her arms and legs for cuts and scratches. Finding only a few minor areas she takes a deep breath.

Watching her, Ashley decides to get the answers to her questions out of the way.

"So. You want to explain what you were doing buried up in the dirt playing with snakes and Philistine soldiers?"

"No, but I guess I will. I was watching the camp to see if there was any way to sneak in to get the Seal from Goliath's shield."

"Paige! Do you even have any idea what those Philistine soldiers could have done to you had they caught you?"

"Yes. I was being careful until the side of the mountain fell in on top of me."

"You could have been killed."

Tears filled Ashley's eyes.

"I'm okay. There was something else too."

"Something else?"

"Yes. I think your shadow of evil was there."

"Oh Paige! Was he frightening? Tell me what happened."

"I felt that coldness that washes over you and then this feeling of hopelessness like someone dropped a net over me. Then the snake was there. I had not even noticed a snake being there at all. I think I would have noticed something like that, don't you? Ugh!"

"A serpent. That's his most used form."

"He's a snake in the grass alright. A dead one thanks to that soldier. He had his arm right under my nose practically. He smelled so bad that I gagged. I was so scared. I held my breath and then the tears started rolling down my face. If he hadn't moved his arm when he did he would have felt the tears and discovered me. I never felt so alone in all my life. Like it was just me alone in the universe."

"Thank the Lord he didn't find you. And you've got to know you are never alone. Never."

"Oh and I almost lost it when he said…" What is that awful smell… like sheep dung.". I wanted to yell at him that sheep smelled great compared to him."

"Sheep dung?"

Ashley started sniffing her cloak.

"We can't smell it. The awful smell has burnt out the smell sensors in our nose."

Both girls laughed.

Ashley stopped laughing and looked at Paige all serious like.

"I know I'm not telling you anything you don't know or hadn't thought already but please listen to me. We are caught in a place no one can rescue us from. All we have really is each other. Attempting to do what we have been asked to do alone is a horrible thought. For myself, I readily admit I can't do it without you. You are not alone. You have me. Together we can do this. If one of us could do this alone I believe God would have sent only one. He didn't. he sent us both. When we try separately to find or get the Seal we fail. Please don't leave me behind again.

"OH… like… united we stand, divided we fall, and if our backs should ever be against the wall, we'll be together. Together you and I."

"Yeah. That's an old song. But it's true. Are we together in this?"

"Yes, together. So, Ashley. What is our plan for getting the Seal from Goliath's shield?"

"I've been thinking about that. When David kills Goliath, I think he puts the armor in his tent. I wish I could remember what the Bible actually says about that but I can't. We just have to find his tent and find a way to get in to look for the shield, without getting caught."

"Piece of cake! When does David do the deed?"

"Any day now. Could be today."

"Well, I feel like a nap is in order. I was awake most of the night and up early. Wake me up if the excitement starts. We do have tickets for this event with the best seats in the house. I for one don't want to miss the show."

"Sure. I wish I had a good book to read. This could become boring."
Paige yawned and snuggled into her blankets.

"Ummm, boring, yes."

And then she was asleep, leaving Ashley with her thoughts and fears.

"Lord, we definitely need your help with this. Thank you for being my Savior. I am never alone. I never feel alone. You are always there. Please show Paige your love. Show her that she needs You. Take care of and protect us from harm. Watch over my family until I get home. Amen."

Chapter 31

The ground shaking woke Ashley up as she had fallen asleep under the warm sunshine. Reaching over to Paige she wakes her up too.

"Wake up Paige! Goliath is on the move again. Let's get to our front seats. David may respond."

"Wouldn't he have stopped here first to see us?"

"I don't think so. David is a Protector. I think Goliath's call is too great for him to ignore. The Bible describes the story wonderfully. I remember it being one of my favorites as a small child.

His oldest brother was a jerk to him. David's path was fashioned by God. The Bible says David was the apple of God's eyes. He made a lot of mistakes and bad decisions but we all do that and yet God still loves us. You have to admit after having spent so much time with him on the mountain that David's heart is in the right place."

"Doesn't the Bible say something about God looking at the heart and not a person's appearance?"

"Yes. At David's anointing. He told Samuel He looked at the heart not the appearance."

"Do you think David will remember us when we are gone?"

"Do you think we will remember David when we get home?"

"My answer to both questions is I hope so."

"Me too Paige, me too."

They managed to crawl into the crevice of the two rocks when they heard Goliath once again.

"Am I a dog, that you come to me with sticks?"

"Ashley look! It's David. Oh, he seems so little compared to Goliath."

"You're right Paige. But we know how this story ends. Watch."

"Come to me, and I will give your flesh to the birds of the sky and the beasts of the field."

David replied.

"You come to me with a sword, a spear, and a javelin, but I come to you in the name of the Lord of hosts, the God of the armies of Israel, whom you have taunted. This day the Lord will deliver you up into my hands, and I will strike you down and remove your head from you. And I will give the dead bodies of the army of the Philistines this day to the birds of the sky and the wild beasts of the earth, that all the earth may know that there is a God in Israel, and that all this assembly may know that the Lord does not deliver by sword or by spear, for the battle is the Lord's and He will give you into our hands."

Goliath started toward David and then David ran toward him. While David was running toward Goliath he pulled a stone from his bag placing it in the sling and swung it around and around and then letting it go. His aim was true and the stone struck Goliath deep in the forehead. Goliath's eyes widened with shock and disbelief as he fell face first onto the ground. He never once moved again.

David ran to Goliath and picked up his sword using it to finish the kill. He then used the sword to cut off Goliath's head.

All of a sudden there was complete chaos on the battlefield. The Philistines turned and ran. The Israelites issued a mighty yell and ran after the Philistines.

"Ashley! Look!" Paige pointed to the valley.

A man was running toward the Philistine's camp holding a large shield in his hands.

"The shield carrier. He has Goliath's shield! We have to stop him. How Paige are we going to stop that man?"

"Run Ashley! We have to take the shortcut to the Philistine's camp." Paige started running to the left of the mountain.

"You mean go back to the dirt pit I rescued you from?" Ashley ran behind Paige.

"Yes! I hope that soldier got that snake. I do not want to see it again. Hurry Ashley. We do not have much time."

"I know. The Israelites raid the camp when they get tired of chasing the Philistines."

The girls run up to the side of the mountain facing the Philistines camp. They peered over the side to check the activity of the camp. All was quiet. It looked like no one was there. Both girls knew it was just a matter of minutes before the camp was full of Israelite soldiers plundering the camp. Following Ashley down the side of the mountain Paige swallowed hard as fear gripped her throat. They made it safely to the ground knowing their luck was running out.

"Paige!" Ashley pointed to a man running into a tent with the shield in his arms.

Ashley took off running toward the tent with Paige at her heels.

Their adrenaline running full force prevented them from using caution before entering the tent. They ran straight into the tent.

It was a toss up who was the most surprised by their presence, the girls or the shield carrier.

The shield carrier however reacted first.

With his fist around the hilt of a sword he shouted,

"Halt! Come no further. Drop your weapons. I said drop your weapons!"

The girls looked at the man in complete shock.

Ashley recovered quickly. Grabbing Paige's hand, she said.

"We… we do not have any weapons sir."

"Lower your head covering." With his sword he made a motion toward their heads.

With fear in their eyes and sinking hearts the girls looked at each other and knew they were running out of time.

Chapter 32

They dropped their hoodies from their heads.

"Girls! You're just girls. Do you both know what danger you are in?" the man had a puzzled look on his face.

"Yes sir. We need to retrieve a stolen object. Once we have that we can go home. Can you help us and not kill us please? We are not your enemy or a threat to you."

Paige nearly choked on her own tongue as Ashley spoke to the man.

"Stolen object?"

"Yes, it's on your champion's shield."

"There are many stones on the shield. To which do you refer?" He pulled up the shield for the girls to see.

Paige saw the Seal in the middle of a fortune of precious gems. Her gasp was the only sound in the tent.

Ashley looked closely at the big man standing before them. He was big with wide shoulders and strong arms. His hair was to his shoulders. His face was nice but his eyes were an amazing shade of green. It was his eyes that held her complete attention. He searched her soul with his eyes. He questioned her with his eyes. He tested her with his eyes.

"We only want the silver one in the center of the shield."

Paige grabbed her arm to indicate they needed more but Ashley shook her head.

"The silver one in the center sir if we may. You better hurry with whatever you came here to do because the Israelites will return to this camp and will leave nothing undiscovered."

The man used a dagger to pop the Seal from the shield and handed it to Ashley.

"Thank you, sir." Ashley bowed her head to the man and grabbing Paige's hand pulled her toward the door.

"Don't forget to cover your heads and thanks for the warning."

"Thank you for the help sir. Will you tell me your name?"

"Gabriel." He smiled for the first time. Ashley smiled back and nodded and turned to go.

Ashley tucked the Seal in the pocket of her cloak and started running towards the side of the mountain that they came down on. Once there she started her climb. Paige was right behind her.

As they climbed they heard the shouts and yells of the Israelite soldiers as they came into the camp. The shouts sounded closer than either of the girls wanted but they kept climbing. Once on firm ground again they took off for their camp. Running for all they were worth.

Sounding out of breath, as she ran, Paige questioned Ashley.

"Why did that Philistine shield carrier help us so willingly? Didn't you find that strange?"

Ashley was out of breath too and didn't answer, but she did smile, as if she had a secret. And she did.

Just as they got to their boulders a soldier stepped out from between the rocks. Both girls screamed.

"It's me David."

"David, you scared us half to death. We hoped we would see you before we left. We found the Seal. We saw you kill Goliath. That was really something."

"Paige, slow down. You will lose your breath. Are you both alright? Ashley?"

"Yes David. I'm glad you came to check on us. We will miss you. Thank you for all you have taught us. I wish we could spend more time with you and learn more. I hope you will be allowed to remember us and us you. You are truly a good, kind and gentle young man. You will have a great life. Don't ever change. People are not so different from your sheep you know. They walk on two legs and can talk back but still the same. When you make mistakes, and you will, just beg forgiveness and keep going. Our God is a God of second chances. Thank you again for everything."

Tears sparkled in Ashley's eyes.

"Yes David, we will even miss your sheep." Paige laughed and turned her head to hide her tears.

Then she screamed, finding them surrounded by Israelite soldiers.

David tried to back the soldiers up but they were too hyped up with the chase and Goliath's death. The path to the two rocks where they watched David kill Goliath was open and Ashley grabbed Paige's hand and they slowly backed up toward them. Ashley's thoughts were if they could get to the rocks while the soldiers were distracted by David they could hide. This however was not an option because all of the soldiers were not distracted and they crowded into the girls, pushing them back towards the side of the mountain.

Ashley and Paige were so terrorized they did not realize that they were continually getting closer to the edge of the mountain. The drop off insured death to anyone who was so unfortunate as to fall from the top.

David turned to check on the girls and was immediately terrified to see them both at the edge.

David's look so impressed on Ashley that she turned to Paige to check on her, forgetting that she held her hand tight in her own.

Ashley's eyes met Paige's eyes just as they went over the edge of the mountain. Their screams filled the valley.

David ran to the edge as he heard them both scream.

"Michael!!!"

Then absolute silence.

No sound came from all the soldiers looking over the edge to the empty valley below. No sound from the two girls who completely disappeared into thin air. No sound at all.

No sound except…. David's laughter resounding up to Heaven.

Chapter 33

Ashley lifted her head to look directly into Paige's eyes.

She and Paige were laying on their stomachs on a dirt surface, facing each other. Beyond them standing to the side was an old man. To say he was surprised to see them was hard to tell as his face did not change expressions at all. Getting ready to alert Paige of the man's presence, Ashley began to say.

"Paige." Paige however was already speaking.

"Ashley? Uhh, Ashley how many pads did we say a sheep has?"

Keeping her eyes on the man Ashley replied.

"Two I think."

"And the bigger print with four toes and a center pad?"

"A lion."

"A lion?" Paige raised her eyes from the prints on the dirt floor they were laying on and looked right into the eyes of the largest lion she had ever seen.

"Uhh Ashley. Make that plural. Lions as in twelve of them. Holy crap Ashley we are in a lion's den."

"Yes, and I think this man here is Daniel."

Printed in the United States
By Bookmasters